CW01082465

THE
BRADFELL
CONSPIRACY

Being An Interactive Mystery In Which
The Reader Attempts To Find a Friend
And Solve a Murder In An Amusing Yet
Annoying City Without Losing Their Life

Samuel Isaacson

Dedication

To everyone who loved Portsrood Forest as
much as I do

Other books by the

same author

Escape From Portsrood Forest

THE ENTRAM EPIC
The Altimer
New Gaia
Solar War

FOR CHILDREN
You're a Wizard!

Acknowledgements

My gratitude must begin with you, that most special person who's put the time, money and effort into starting to read this book. The feeling of creating something that other people appreciate is a very special one, and you make that happen: thank you.

Particular thanks need to go to James Spearing, whose personal encouragement and challenge I've always appreciated, and whose work on *My Gamebook Adventures* is a great service to the gamebook community as a whole.

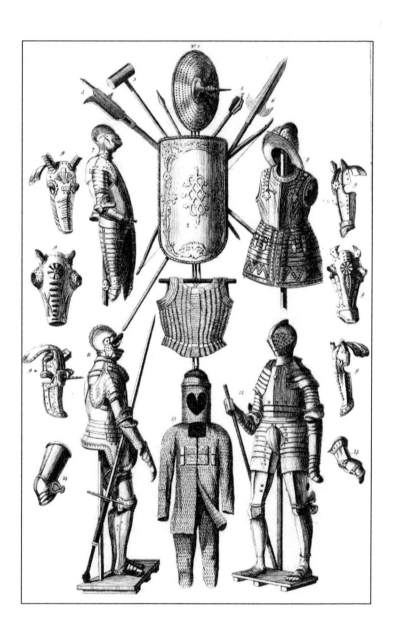

Introduction

elcome to Bradfell. Thank you so much for visiting! As you are about to discover, it will prove far more difficult to escape than it was to enter.

Bradfell is a city that will probably get on your nerves, populated by a variety of people who incomprehensibly seem to love it. Some of them want to help you, some of them want to help themselves and you might play a part in that, and some of them are only ever going to get in your way. By the time you've explored it, you'll have met kind lawbreakers, unethical lawkeepers, chaotic monsters and all sorts of other riffraff you'd expect to meet in a fantasy city.

You are about to enter that city, because *you* are the one written about in this book. As you read, you will encounter options to travel in different directions and take various actions, which will direct you to read the numbered sections throughout the book. As you flick between the pages, your story will develop, as will the world around you.

This will happen particularly through having various encounters, picking up and using items, and discovering information. Some of this may be helpful in finding your way out, and some of it will lead you to a premature end, which will typically be amusing and/or unpleasant.

The city isn't huge, but it will take you time to travel from one end to another as you navigate the criss-crossing streets and other spaces in the city. There are landmarks and street names to help you find your way, but you're still likely to find yourself wandering around, looking for somewhere you could *swear* you went this way to get to last time, and at times the city contains unannounced dangers that will confuse you further.

Don't say I didn't warn you.

As you explore, make a detailed map of the city and take plenty of notes. And if you're really stuck, make sure to visit the website, **https://www.IsaacsonAuthor.com** for clues and errata, and for a delightful, full-size colour map of Bradfell. I promise, it is possible to solve the city's mysteries and ultimately to get out, so see if you can uncover the city's secrets and calculate the optimal route. You'll know you've done it properly when you've completed every side quest, and visited every pub, temple, garden and shop.

It might take you a while.

Codewords

The book uses codewords to keep track of certain decisions you have made and things you have experienced. You may find it helpful to use the list below to keep track of any codewords you gather on your travels.

❏ Alexandre
❏ Barsad
❏ Bernard
❏ Carton
❏ Cly
❏ Cruncher
❏ Darnay
❏ Defarge
❏ Ernest
❏ Evremonde
❏ Foulon
❏ Gabelle
❏ Gaspard
❏ Jacques
❏ Jarvis
❏ Jourdan
❏ Launay
❏ Lorry
❏ Lucie
❏ Manette
❏ Pross
❏ Solomon
❏ Stryver
❏ Theophile

Tickboxes

Some sections include a box to tick, indicating that you have been there before. When your adventure concludes and you would like to replay, it will be important to rub those ticks out. You may therefore find the complete list of tickbox sections below helpful, either as a way of keeping track or to help you find them all.

❏ 41
❏ 57
❏ 58
❏ 71
❏ 130
❏ 131
❏ 135
❏ 140
❏ 162
❏ 198

❏ 213
❏ 234
❏ 275
❏ 295
❏ 320
❏ 327
❏ 344
❏ 351
❏ 375

Notes

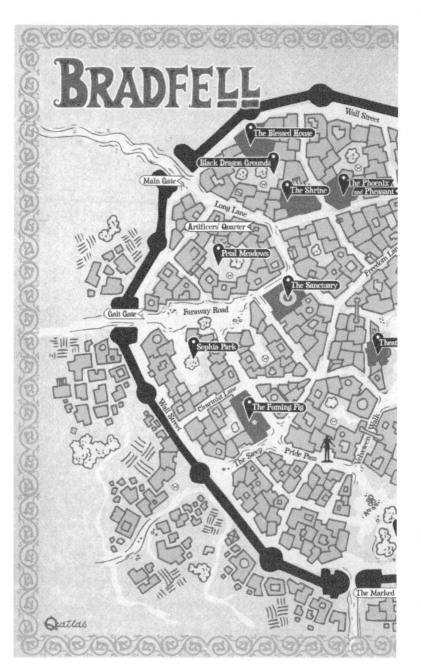

BRADFELL

Wall Street

The Blessed House

Black Dragon Grounds

Main Gate

The Shrine

The Phoenix and Pheasant

Long Lane

Artificers' Quarter

Petal Meadows

Freedom Lane

The Sanctuary

Gait Gate

Faraway Road

Theat

Sophia Park

Clearmist Lane

Wall Street

The Fuming Fig

Velveteen Walk

The Sweep

Pride Pass

The Marked

Qatlas

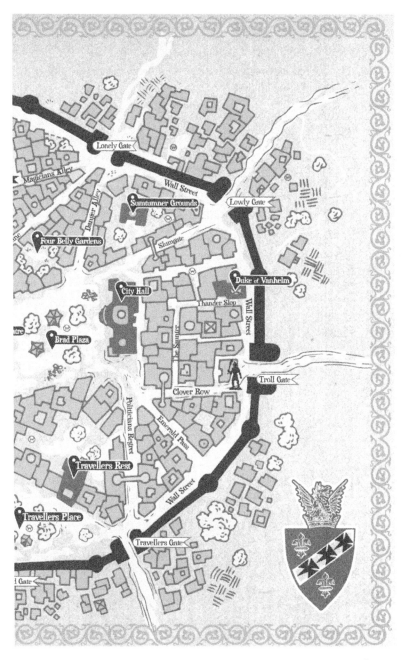

Alphabet reference

You may find this table helpful for solving some of the riddles you encounter as you traverse the city.

A	B	C	D	E	F	G	H	I	J
1	2	3	4	5	6	7	8	9	10

K	L	M	N	O	P	Q	R	S	T
11	12	13	14	15	16	17	18	19	20

U	V	W	X	Y	Z
21	22	23	24	25	26

"Free roam" mode

Sometimes, you just want to get lost in a fictional city without the threat of death around every turn. If you're in that sort of mood, begin your journey with the following combination of codewords, and all tickboxes checked.

- ☐ Alexandre
- ☑ Barsad
- ☐ Bernard
- ☐ Carton
- ☐ Cly
- ☑ Cruncher
- ☐ Darnay
- ☐ Defarge
- ☐ Ernest
- ☐ Evremonde
- ☐ Foulon
- ☐ Gabelle
- ☐ Gaspard
- ☐ Jacques
- ☑ Jarvis
- ☐ Jourdan
- ☐ Launay
- ☐ Lorry
- ☐ Lucie
- ☐ Manette
- ☐ Pross
- ☐ Solomon
- ☑ Stryver
- ☐ Theophile

Background

Trade deals fall into a special sort of bucket in your mind, entitled: Dull And Easies. As one of the Portsrood Protectors, you are called upon by the good Queen Sophia to carry out all sorts of quests, and they tend to fall into three buckets.

First of all, there are the Adventures. These are your run-of-the-mill, defeat some goblins and save the member of royalty sort of quests. They're fun, well-paid, and have a defined end date.

Next, there are the Suicide Missions. These are the ones you farm out to the newbies. Certain failure, almost-certain death, but it gives a good story to tell. You've gone on enough quests in your time to be able to sniff out a Suicide Mission from a mile off.

And then there are Dull And Easies. These are the sorts of quests you hope to retire into. They're not too challenging, tend to drag on, and most of the action seems be in other people's hands.

Trade deals sit squarely in this camp.

So, when the opportunity to go on a quest to accompany a trade deal party heading out from Portsrood to Bradfell, you feigned a headache, and then got dropped in it by Sir Tostig, along with Sir Julia, who had an actual headache. Queen Sophia had raised her eyebrows at Sir Tostig's suggestion, and sent the three of you along with Sir Engelard on the quest, saying that it's of strategic importance to the kingdom. Of course it is.

And that's how you found yourself at a banquet in a delightful old stately home called Sumtumner Manor in the city of Bradfell, celebrating the prosperity a trade deal could bring.

Ah yes, the only good part of Dull And Easies. Nothing to do, but food and drink tends to get thrown in. The Council of Bradfell seemed to be pleased with the whole idea, and everyone had a lovely evening, even if it did seem to get a bit out of hand towards the end.

The high beams and hanging banners within the building gave a pleasant environment for your rich meal, and you had a good conversation with the mayor, Heidi Hillestad, who expressed her admiration of Queen Sophia's latest approach to taxes, which meant nothing to you.

Keegan, a man with a love for battle, on the other hand, was easier to talk to, even though he left early saying something about a sense of duty.

And then there was an overly friendly and tactile man that everyone called Husband Graham. He seemed to be friends with everyone, but was a bit too much if you're being honest, and you were grateful for the distraction of the never-ending food to stop you from having to speak to him for too long.

And now, it's the morning after, and your head is actually alright. The City Hall – a venue halfway between your rooms for the night and yesterday's festivities – is hosting a celebratory breakfast this morning, so that's where you head first thing. The plan is, well, dull and easy: eat until you're full, take possession of the signed paperwork in an over-engineered ceremony, and set off back towards Portsrood around lunchtime.

You arrive at the City Hall in good time, and tuck into the fare that has been laid out for you. Regional guinea fowl, seafood brought in fresh from the Sapphire Sea and locally-grown potatoes adorn various platters alongside plenty of rustic bread and local ale. You appreciate the effort they've gone to, and sit down to your meal, already looking forward to returning to Portsrood Castle.

While you're eating, your fellow knights from Portsrood join you, greeting you jovially as they enter.

Well, Sir Engelard and Sir Tostig do. Sir Julia doesn't, although this doesn't worry you too much. She's often late for breakfast, particularly when you're on tour.

When breakfast is over, you and the other Protectors enter the main meeting chamber.

Turn to **1**.

1

Heidi is now sitting on a throne, looking far more respectable than she did the previous evening, although her regal act feels inappropriate given her humble position in contrast to your Queen. As she invites you to come and shake her hand, she allows hers to linger a few seconds longer than you'd like, although you know it's good to keep the peace at times like this and so you say nothing.

The optimism surrounding your first day has been maintained, and the small talk from the previous evening continues without too much effort.

"Well," Heidi announces with the greatest aplomb she can muster, "all that's left is for us to read the details of the trade agreement through and sign it, and then the four of you can be presented with – wait, where's the other one?"

The three of you try to cover your amusement with a look of surprise.

"Oh, um, where could she possibly be?" declares Sir Tostig, calling on his greatest acting abilities. All of you already know the answer: Sir Julia will be asleep in bed at the Travellers Rest, most likely draped across a trembling young man, terrified to move in case he wakes her to find that she still has energy left. This is not the first time that Sir Julia has not turned up for a meeting before noon.

"We will have to mount a search!" proclaims Sir Engelard, his eyes twinkling with adventure. You and Sir Tostig boldly nod, already marching towards the door.

Heidi, stunned to silence for a moment, shakes her head as if to wake herself from a trance, and nods.

"Yes, you go and get her, and the Council will get the paperwork seen to. We'll be over in Sumtumner Manor again if you need us."

Will you search around the City Hall before leaving (turn to **358**), or head directly out into Brad Plaza (turn to **131**)?

2

Politicians Court is the name given to a funny-shaped corner of Brad Plaza alongside the City Hall, where a group of strange folk adorned in leaves seem to have gathered around a flimsy tree. You try to ascertain what they're getting so flustered about but make no progress on that front.

A door, long-since bricked up, is set into the wall here, through which the elders of Bradfell used to enter the City Hall, while the general townsfolk would be ushered in through the main entrance.

Why an entrance intended for political leaders would be subject to fewer security requirements is beyond you, and why the choice was subsequently made to remove the distinction

between them and the commoners flummoxes you further.

Still feeling slightly confused, you take in your surroundings. Three roads lead down the hill in different directions from this point, while Politicians Court itself provides access to Brad Plaza, the main meeting point of the city.

East: Clover Row   Turn to **171**

South-east: Emerald Pass	Turn to **346**
South: Politicians Regret	Turn to **246**
North-west: Brad Plaza	Turn to **8**

3

The road steadily bends around to the south at a point where it has been widened to allow for vehicles to manoeuvre more easily. You consider for a moment stopping to help a confused-looking local scratching her head as she tries to convince a horse to reverse and turn simultaneously, deciding that you're likely to only make matters worse.

A short time later, you arrive at another junction (turn to **237**).

4

You reach the point at which Clear Mist Lane, leading down the hill to the south-west, meets Dragontoothache Passage, climbing away to the north-east. Fabled Alley takes you around the side of Bradfell hill to the north, skirting Sophia Park, while Grace Way offers to take you south-east, along the wall of the Fuming Fig.

From this angle, the Fuming Fig could look like a half-decent inn; its windows are almost transparent, and the sign that juts out over the crossroads seems to have been freshly painted.

Into the Fuming Fig	Turn to **336**
North: Fabled Alley	Turn to **17**

North-east: Dragontoothache
Passage   Turn to **134**
South-east: Grace Way   Turn to **170**
South-west: Clear Mist Lane   Turn to **62**

5

If you have the codeword *Jarvis*, turn immediately to **114**.

If not, turn to **90**.

6

You can feel your spirit getting calmer as you take the first few steps away from the pretentious T-junction that defines so much about how much you despise this city. Managing to ignore the murals on either side, you hurry along the street until you emerge into Travellers Place (turn to **36**).

7

You can't help feeling that whoever designed this narrow alley intended it to be accessed from the top rather than the bottom as you find yourself slipping up its oddly-shaped steps. Halfway up, a pair of doorsteps that face each other force you to have to jump over, and you emerge from the other side (turn to **58**).

8

If you have the codeword *Defarge*, turn immediately to **398**.

If not, turn to **242**.

9

Following the patterns of the cobbles to avoid tripping, you keep on running until you are sure they are no longer behind you.

Carefully pulling into a doorway to look in every direction you survey the scene, and once you're sure you've lost them you take a deep breath, and get your bearings (turn to **109**).

10

You barely get on board before the carriage has started moving, and the driver grumpily gees on the horses, which trot barely faster than you could walk, making stops at each of the gates.

Where will you ask to get off?

Gait Gate	Turn to **344**
Lonely Gate	Turn to **108**
Lowly Gate	Turn to **226**
Main Gate	Turn to **25**
Marked Gate	Turn to **201**
Travellers Gate	Turn to **204**
Troll Gate	Turn to **80**

11

You come to, tied up in what looks like a cellar, surrounded by casks of various shapes and sizes. Alongside you, Sir Engelard and Sir Tostig seem to have joined you, the three of you tied to chairs.

"Hmm," says Sir Tostig, a smile still present on his face. "How are we going to get out of this then?"

You notice some sort of upturned sledge lying against one wall, its blades offering you a way to cut your ties if you could get over there.

Alternatively, Sir Engelard points out that you most likely have captors, and you could try to get their attention by saying you need the toilet, tricking them into untying you.

Sir Tostig has a different idea, in the form of tipping your chair upside down on top of his, enabling you to reach high enough to kick open a window and get the attention of someone passing by outside.

Which will you choose? Will you try to jump your chair over to the corner to cut your ties (turn to **240**), try to attract the attention of a captor (turn to **268**), or flip upside down on top of Sir Tostig's chair (turn to **355**)?

12

A few paces into the alley and you notice a slight glow emanating from a doorway just ahead.

"Erm," says Sir Tostig, "I don't like the look of this."

"Oh, I don't know," offers Sir Engelard, a tone of reasonableness in his voice, "it's like I always say: unknown light – treasure's in sight!"

You don't think you've ever heard him say that. Will you turn around (turn to **270**) or continue ahead to investigate the source of the light (turn to **147**)?

13

If you have the codeword *Defarge*, turn immediately to **398**.

If not, turn to **244**.

14

The steps descend, the wear of many generations obvious beneath your feet as you find your boots slipping into the grooves that so many have formed before you. A junction greets you as you reach the bottom (turn to **144**).

15

Marching down the hill you begin to wonder to yourself whether the group of labourers that laid the final cobbles here weren't specifically tasked with making it as precarious a journey as possible.

A smooth hill you could understand, and even steps, while over-engineered, would at least be understandable. But the lunacy of discordant stones that feels like an obstacle course as you descend is as much as you think anyone can take. Then again, the elderly gentleman who seems to sprint past you, navigating every unpredictable step along the way, suggests that perhaps you're the one with the problem.

Grumbling to yourself, you reach Wall Street at the bottom of the hill (turn to **109**).

16

The long road known as Fabled Alley is one of the better kept of Bradfell, with large houses and larger gardens boasting views over the clusters of trees scattered across Sophia Park to the south. After some time you reach the next junction (turn to **234**).

17

The sunlight reflecting off the pristine paving slabs at your feet offers a stark contrast to your experience of most of the rest of the city.

You are just considering that this road must boast some of the more respectable inhabitants of Bradfell when a dusty fellow emerges from a garden gate ahead of you. Naturally you cross the road to avoid being too close to him, and continue until you reach a T-junction (turn to **135**).

18

"What are you doing here?" the author says, surprised. "Wait, let me check...no, there's no way you've been sent here. You're not just flicking through the pages at random, are you?"

An odd sensation of guilty excitement tickles you, followed immediately by an understated amusement as the author pinpoints your experience. Perhaps he is an undervalued creative genius, leading you to want to buy his other books and tell all of your friends...or perhaps there's a deeper meaning to this nonsense.

The sort of person who gets to the third paragraph of a section that clearly has no bearing on the storyline must have a particular wiring; have you ever considered writing a gamebook? The author seems to be willing to help you. Why not contact him referencing this section, and see what happens?

19

Leaving the theatre behind doesn't remove you from the theatre district, and if anything the people around become even stranger the further you get from Brad Plaza.

Doing everything you can to avoid eye contact – or any sort of contact for that matter – you arrive at another junction (turn to **98**).

20

"Yes, Husband Graham said you might like to," the wife murmurs, half under her breath, as she bends to pull a handful of herbs with leaves shaped like teardrops in a blue-purple hue.

In contrast to the other plants in the garden these seem to be odourless, which seems odd, even when you crush them. From experience, however, you conclude that they may come in handy later. Taking random items on the off chance they'll be the one thing standing between you and victory is part and parcel of being a hero, after all.

Record the codeword *Ernest*.

Speak to Husband Graham	Turn to **275**
Get a blessing from a wife	Turn to **303**
Leave into Black Dragon Grounds	Turn to **47**
Leave onto Wall Street	Turn to **194**

21

You are standing outside the door that leads into the Legion Crushers, and can't help glancing towards it for a moment. As you look up, an old woman walking past mutters, whether to you or to herself you can't be sure:

"The winners receive a magic mark, that's right. The wise woman welcomes them, that's right. Thrice Meadow Lookout, that's the place, that's right."

She strolls away, still muttering to herself. Do you head on to the south (turn to **28**), or to the north (turn to **271**)?

22

You are in Sophia Park, the large, spacious green area named after your beloved Queen. While you consider the area bearing her name, you can't help your mind resting on your memories of her.

Queen Sophia is everything you could want in a royal. Of course, she's well bred – that goes without saying – she's also extremely rich, and quite handsome to boot.

Your chest swelling with pride, you take in the park, which is full of people milling around in groups, clustering under trees to tell stories and sing songs, while young lovers scuttle along in pairs around you.

After enjoying the space, which feels more like Portsrood than any other part of Bradfell you've visited so far, you decide to leave.

North-east: Faraway Road	Turn to **249**
East: Clear Mist Lane	Turn to **234**
South: Wall Street	Turn to **130**
North-west: Gait Gate	Turn to **344**

23

You explain the experience you had in the crowd and the way you immediately felt, and Pratt instantly rolls his eyes.

"Oh, it'll be that fool Powell Powell, up to his old tricks again. You did the right thing coming to see me. He has this idea that he can get people hooked on this psychedelic potion he's concocted. His idea is that by giving you a first dose for free you'll come back for more. Standard business practice, but he's so shady about the way he goes about it I don't know how anyone finds him for a second try."

He turns around and opens a cupboard, and then stops himself.

"I don't suppose you'd rather I introduced you to him so you can buy some-" he sees the look on your face and immediately turns back to the cupboard, clearing his throat unnecessarily.

"Here you go, drink this," he continues as he turns back, passing you a small vial. "No charge, I know you're here on the queen's business. I don't suppose you can put in a good word for me?" He sees your face again. "Never mind."

You drink the liquid. Remove the codeword *Pross*.

Thanking Bottomley Pratt for his truly invaluable help, you leave onto Long Lane. Will you head to the north-west (turn to 175), or to the south-east (turn to 213)?

24

Leaving the statue and everything it represents behind you, you continue along the road, wondering how anyone in this confounded town manages to build up enough motivation to even get out of bed in the morning.

Becoming aware that the unsightly smiles on the faces of these poor people around you is beginning to make you feel a bit sick, you arrive at a junction (turn to **222**).

25

Main Gate, where you find yourself, was historically the first point of Bradfell most visitors would experience, although since Portsrood took over as the seat of power in the region it has fallen in use, evidenced by the peeling paintwork and lackadaisical expressions on the part of the guards posted at this station, not helped by the rain that is now gathering around your feet.

From here, Long Lane stretches into the distance to the south-east, while Wall Street offers options to follow the city wall in both directions.

"I'd head that way if I were you," the driver of a Gates Carriage mumbles, indicating with his filthy thumb down Long Lane and pulling his cloak around his neck in an attempt to keep out the rain.

Clockwise: Wall Street	Turn to **239**
Anticlockwise: Wall Street	Turn to **391**
South-east: Long Lane	Turn to **53**
Onto the Gates Carriage	Turn to **10**

26

The interior of the Sanctuary of Humility is a disappointment in comparison to the sensory overload of its blazing white exterior. With a distinctly minimalistic vibe, there is no decoration in here whatsoever, and the noise of the crowd outside seems to be muffled somehow, perhaps by magic, leaving you in an uncomfortable state of silence and solitude.

You are about to head for the exit when a Humble Soul, one of the priests inhabiting the Sanctuary, greets you with a deep bow. Her eyes remaining on the floor, she whispers the offer of a meditative experience of simplicity from the cowls of her unbearably unimaginative robe.

Accept the offer of a meditation   Turn to **48**
Leave: Long Lane   Turn to **213**
Leave: Faraway Road   Turn to **320**

27

You swing to your right and feel the satisfying clang of a blade meeting yours. Your knight's training kicking in, you pull your blow before it would decapitate Margaret, but you certainly allow it to connect in a way she won't forget in a hurry.

Pulling your blindfold off, you see Margaret pressing her hand against her neck, blood impossibly spurting everywhere.

"Congratulations, wimp, you managed to nick me. Who's next?"

One of the bystanders reaches over to clap you on the shoulder, and you're handed the traditional spoils of a Privy victory: a pendant containing an ugly piece of grey stone in the shape of a fish.

"Put it on, deary," a wizened, toothless woman sneers at you. "It'll protect you from the pixies."

You hang it around your neck, smiling inwardly at her superstitious nonsense, and thank the room for having you before backing out into the bar.

Record the codeword *Cruncher*.

Speak to the landlord	Turn to **218**
Join the drinkers	Turn to **397**
Leave: Dragontoothache Passage	Turn to **234**
Leave: Pride Pass	Turn to **222**

28

You move south into the shadow of the City Hall, its dirty stone walls rising up to your right, and you don't stop walking until you reach another junction (turn to **185**).

29

You reach the arch that declares that you have reached Travellers Court, in the south-west corner of Brad Plaza.

The bustle of the town square extends away from you to the north-east, ending in the City

Hall, which takes up the whole of the eastern edge of the square. The shimmering blacks and purples of Velveteen Walk lead down the hill to the south-west, while a slim alleyway declaring itself as Dragontoothache Passage leads behind the theatre to the north-west.

Into the City Hall	Turn to **358**
North: Preachers Corner	Turn to **161**
North-east: Slum Corner	Turn to **58**
East: Politicians Court	Turn to **2**
South-west: Velveteen Walk	Turn to **377**
West: Dreary Crescent	Turn to **88**

30

The painting is at quite an angle and so you pull it level to look at it. It portrays a cow standing in a field while in the background someone with unimaginably long hair runs up a hill. You can't tell what the subject of the painting ought to be and are about to leave it when you notice a slight bulge emerging from behind, and pull the painting off the wall.

Set into the wall is a safe! It's locked, and so you will need the right code to break in. If you know the code to get into the safe, take the first, third and fifth digits from it, place them in ascending order, and turn to the section bearing this number.

Otherwise, the safe will have to remain a mystery.

Investigate the body	Turn to **308**

Look out of the window	Turn to **287**
Investigate the tankard of beer	Turn to **163**
Investigate the clothes	Turn to **360**
Leave	Turn to **226**

31

The sounds drifting towards you from the inn on your left making you grateful you're not inside, you continue along the road. The yellow bricks that fill the floor ahead of you conjure up a sense that a thought is knocking on the back of your head, as if a supernatural parallel universe might break in at any second…

You shake the absurd idea from your mind and keep going until the yellow bricks end at the next junction (turn to **95**).

32

Trying to leave the hubbub of Travellers Place behind you, you find yourself joining a stream of young mothers, trailed by countless children, who seem to have made it their job to impede your progress.

Impressing yourself with your patience as you hold your tongue long enough to see them making space for you, you reach a T-junction (turn to **109**).

33

"Right," Edgar says, "let's get down to business then. The butcher, over in Artificers' Quarter, has an assistant. I forget his name. Anyway, he's been helping an associate of mine out with some work, and that associate has recently given me cause to be upset with him.

"I have reason to believe that this apprentice butcher has taken possession of a property deed. What I want you to do is get into his house, find the deed, and bring it to me. Not here though, too close to the you-know-who. I'll wait for you on the corner of The Saunter and Clover Row."

He grabs your arm and pulls you outside, and then points in a vaguely south-easterly direction. "Over there. Go on then, get on with it! See you later, then."

Record the codeword *Evremonde*.

Apparently finished with this conversation, he walks back into the tavern, leaving you alone again (turn to **98**).

34

If you have the codeword *Stryver* and do not have the codeword *Foulon*, turn immediately to **100**.

If you do not have the codeword *Stryver,* or if you have both codewords, turn to **22**.

35

Seething with rage, you look up at the grand statue of Stanothy Pride, who stands looking out towards the coast, an unwelcome expression of peace and humility on his face.

Closing your eyes to stop yourself from screaming at the abomination, a clear whisper suddenly cuts through the sounds of the city around you.

"Psst!"

You turn in the direction of the sound to see a scrawny man in a hat and carrying a cane beckoning you towards him.

"I think I have something you might be interested in – follow me!" he says, then hobbles between two houses on the northern side of the street. When he looks back and you haven't immediately started walking after him, he jogs back and grabs you by the arm with an inexplicable strength.

"Oops, sorry," he says as he pulls you away, "magic," as if that single word explains everything. He leads you through a narrow alleyway to an alcove, where he turns back towards you, leaning against the wall.

"Phew! Right! You're going to like this," he says, his enthusiasm embarrassing him. "I've always been a fan of the Protectors. Big fan! Really big! And..." he leans forward in a conspiratorial manner, "I think I could help you. I've crafted a magical item. Maybe the magicalest

item ever! That's what they say, anyway. That rhymes. A beautiful – *beautiful, I say! Ha!* – a beautiful necklace. And I'd like to give it to you, but it'll need activating, and here's my quandary. I'm good at the old magicraft, but not so good at the old, you know…"

He starts to whistle and twist his finger against his temple as if to signify something, but you can't make out what. "So here's how, if you help me, I can help you. I've just brought on a new assistant, who's written out this sequence for me and then popped out for the day. Any chance you can help?"

He hands you a scrap of paper, on which is written the following:

101 112 131 415 161 718

"I really need to work out what comes next. What would the next three digits be?"

If you can work out what the next three digits would be, turn to that section number.

If not, turn to **173**.

36

Travellers Place offers the first experience most visitors have of Bradfell, and it's perfectly pleasant, as things in this dump of a city go.

Trees have been allowed to grow at various points around the large, triangular, open space, and a fountain, decorated with various carvings, sits in the centre of it. Locals clearly use it as a meeting spot, and several are sharing recent town gossip, which you imagine will relate to you in some way.

The Travellers Rest sits at the midway point of the north-east edge of the Place, known locally as the Rest Parade, while the west edge is known as the Meadow Parade. The point that the Rest Parade and the Meadow Parade meet provides access to Velveteen Walk, which climbs the hill to Brad Plaza, and Pride Pass, running almost perpendicular to it.

The Meadow Parade stretches down to the Marked Gate at the south, split halfway along by Thrice Meadow Lookout, while the city wall here is lined with small traders, selling useless bracelets, unlucky charms, and flavourless pies.

Investigate the fountain	Turn to **193**
Into the Travellers Rest	Turn to **198**
North-east: Velveteen Walk	Turn to **359**
South-west: Marked Gate	Turn to **201**
South-east: Travellers Gate	Turn to **204**
West: Thrice Meadow Lookout	Turn to **84**
West: Pride Pass	Turn to **399**

37

It's a short walk from Shepherds Hill around the corner building, but that doesn't stop it taking time, as the optical illusion of the unpredictable animals carved into its walls seems to temporarily hypnotise you.

Trying to ignore the nonsensical creatures and the locals' ability to go about their days as normal with the nightmarish beings staring down at them, you hurry to Lowly Gate (turn to **226**).

38

You are at a T-junction on Long Lane, not far from Brad Plaza. Freedom Lane leads away to the north-east in a straight line, and it surprises you that the lack of people on the road allows a clear view of one of the town gates at the bottom of the hill.

In fact, crowds seem to surround you in every other direction, and everyone seems to be paying careful attention to not go past a sign attached to a building on the left-hand wall saying "Warning. Do Not Pass."

On the eastern corner of Freedom Lane, two of the city watch stand on either side of the front door of the home of Keegan, the now deceased Chief of BLEED.

Into Keegan's home	Turn to **289**
North-east: Freedom Lane	Turn to **283**
South-east: Preachers Corner	Turn to **161**
North-west: Long Lane	Turn to **199**

39

The sign at the bottom of the street declares it to be Emerald Pass. Just as you are looking up the hill, your arm is suddenly grabbed by an unseen attacker, and a vial is smashed against your helmet, causing a sweet-tasting liquid to cascade down your face, into your nose and mouth.

"Ha!" your assailant cries as they fly into the crowds and out of sight, "Welcome to my special place! Be seeing you!"

You desperately try to wipe away the surprise substance, knowing full well you swallowed some and expecting to feel, well, *something*, but no effect appears to be forthcoming. In any case, you definitely think it would be worth seeing someone about whatever it is that's just happened to you.

Record the codeword *Pross*, and turn to **333**.

40

You set your sights on the crest of the hill and make your way up, the delicate crunching of your plate mail commentating your ascent while the sounds of the gate activity behind you merges into the sounds of Brad Plaza ahead. After some time walking, you reach the top (turn to **58**).

41 ☐

If the box above is ticked, turn immediately to **151**.

If not, put a tick in it now and turn to **96**.

42

Your drop into the water isn't far, and you're treading water within a few moments. You search around the surface of the water for anything out of the ordinary but everything seems normal.

It is only then that you wonder how you will get out – the rope is too far above you. You try getting a grip on the sides, but they are slippery and you can't make any progress.

A sudden shift in the shadows causes you to look up, just in time to see the rope tumble down the shaft towards you and splash into the water by your side. The next thing you see is two pairs of arms leaning out over the opening to place a large cover over it. You try to shout, but are unceremoniously plunged into darkness.

You're trapped.

Thoughts race through your mind in an attempt to construct an escape plan, but nothing seems to work, and then a light in the water beneath you lifts your spirits. Perhaps you've discovered a secret tunnel?

No, it turns out that the light belongs to a particularly vicious carnivore that attracts its prey through a glowing orb set into its skull. And you have just been added to its menu.

43

"Oh, right," Oswald says in response to your question. "Well, I might be able to help you, actually, because I'm stuck with this crossword clue. It says, 'A coal-coloured boxer's depression', two words, five letters then three letters. Any idea?"

If you know the answer for Oswald, turn the letters in it into numbers using the code A=1,

B=2, C=3, etc, add them all up and turn to that section number.

If you don't know the answer, you turn to Gwendolyn instead (turn to **46**).

44

Overhanging rooftops and steadily dying plants provide unnecessary shade in this already dull-looking and dirty alleyway, which leads you around the back of the theatre. You keep your head down in case one of the egotistical performers tries to drag you into their narcissism, and don't stop until you reach a T-junction (turn to **145**).

45

She is nimbler than you gave her credit for, and as you move she hears and makes a swift movement in which she grabs you by the ankle.

"Oh, thank you kindly. Now, while you're here, you might be able to help me with something else. You see, I lost a precious necklace. In fact, that was the start of my downfall. I used to be very rich and beautiful if you can believe it, and then misfortune followed betrayal followed some bad choices, and time hasn't done me any favours, as you can see. And that necklace, along with being hideously expensive, carries a magical enchantment. I'd be ever so grateful if you'd find it for me. Some scoundrel probably sold it at Olfric's place on Magicians Alley. Well," at this she stands, stumbling, scrabbling around on the floor to pick up her cloth cap, the few coins in it ricocheting off one another in her trembling hands. "I'm going to head down Faraway Road a bit I think. Better pickings there at this time of day. If you do manage to find it, be a dear and bring it back to me there would you? You'd have my everlasting gratitude, which is probably worth more than you might think."

Record the codeword *Lorry*.

She shuffles off, leaving you slightly bewildered (turn to **158**).

46

"Yes, I might know," Gwendolyn replies when you ask her about the whereabouts of Sir Julia, "and I might be willing to tell you...if you can beat me in combat."

You surely have greater fighting prowess than this angry woman, but something in her eyes tells you she may not be a pushover, and you're hesitant to cause yourself too many problems in your quest.

Will you speak to Oswald instead, in case he's willing to talk (turn to **43**), or will you agree to fight Gwendolyn (turn to **73**)?

47

Black Dragon Grounds is a carefully manicured decorative garden, at the centre of which is a large, clear pool of water, the surface gently rippling thanks to a queer-looking contraption set into its side. Small turtles dance about beneath the surface, accompanying other animals that roam across the lawn yet make no attempt to escape. You suspect magic must be at play here, as if the space is somehow inside and outside at the same time.

The garden is laid out in the form of a skewwhiff cross, as if put in as an afterthought following the introduction of the two large temple buildings to the east, both of which you can access directly from the garden, while a narrow gate in the south-west corner leads out onto Long Lane.

North-east: The Blessed House of
the Husband of Countless Wives
and Sagas of Courageous Acts
With Said Wives   Turn to **115**
South-east: The Shrine of the
Trickle of Wisdom   Turn to **314**
South-west: Long Lane   Turn to **257**

48

The Humble Soul walks you into a private room and sits on the floor, indicating that you do likewise without making eye contact.

"I'd like to invite you to simply notice the room, and notice your body. You are free to simply close your eyes if you wish. Notice your thoughts, and then simply allow them to proceed until they reach their conclusion and your mind is simply still. When you are satisfied that you have reached this state, simply say so. It's simple, isn't it?"

You do as instructed, sceptical at first but before too long beginning to enjoy the stillness. As you do so, you have a sudden revelation that your life as a knight has been one of privilege and entitlement rather than service, and that you have a more effective route to a greater sense of satisfaction and fulfilment.

As if in control of your destiny for the first time, you stand up confidently and declare aloud that you are renouncing everything that has gone before. Your future is now your own, and the rights and responsibilities of the Protectors now belong to the others but not for you.

Your experiences over the next few months are hard, but your newfound faith and focus carry you through to a healthier, happier life as a Humble Soul.

49

This road is long and straight, extending ahead of you for some distance. The delicate sunlight filling the sky reminds you of the world outside this blasted city, and despite the fact that your surroundings at present are reasonably pleasant you find it hard to appreciate them, wishing to return home as quickly as possible.

Eventually, you reach the end of the road where it connects with a wide street heading up and down the hill (turn to **98**).

50

It's as if this terrible version of Portsrood Palace had been designed to make it easy to break into. The passage into the park is dark, and a hole next to the building is large enough for you to walk straight through without being seen. A couple of minutes later, and you're inside.

You navigate through the rooms, accidentally breaking a vase on your way although the state of the whole thing makes you think no-one would notice – in fact, it brings a nice bit of variety to the place now you think about it.

You find the master bedroom as instructed, and the drawer in the dresser opens without the need for a key. You drop in the forged deed, close the drawer, and silently make your way back out again, congratulating yourself on a job well done.

Record the codeword *Solomon* and turn to **340**.

51

The door swings open to reveal the interior of the Phoenix and Pheasant, looking precisely as it did the first time you were here. You think to yourself that Tiffany Palmer was right; even given the state you left it in, the punters are still all exactly where you left them, as if reality has a magnetic space perfectly suited to them.

You nod, slightly awkwardly, to the people in the tavern and back out onto the Shaded Crossroads again (turn to **74**).

52

The final stretch of Long Lane offers passers-by the chance to eat and drink within easy reach of Main Gate, presumably to catch visitors unawares before they've spent any time in this blasted place, although a sudden rumble overhead and the first few drops of rain cause a panic around you as the eating establishments hurry to get their furniture and customers inside.

Your frustration beginning to grow as the rain threatens to saturate you, you stamp on until you reach the gate (turn to **25**).

53

The grim sky above clears a little, revealing bright colours on your left in the sunlight, and as the rain fully lifts, shop owners begin to cautiously emerge and erect small tables for passers-by to sit at while having a drink and a snack.

Slightly envying their ability to just stop, while not actually wanting to partake in the disgusting local produce, you continue until you reach a T-junction (turn to **340**).

54

The fountain is designed to provide easy access to the water, and you scoop some of the cool liquid in your hand.

You take a drink, which you find refreshing, although you have nothing on you that would allow you to take any water with you. Wondering if you could find a container of some sort to gather some into, you ponder where to head next.

Into the Travellers Rest	Turn to **198**
North-east: Velveteen Walk	Turn to **359**
South-east: Travellers Gate	Turn to **204**
South-west: Marked Gate	Turn to **201**
West: Thrice Meadow Lookout	Turn to **84**
West: Pride Pass	Turn to **399**

55

"Black dog!" he shouts. "Of course!"

He scribbles the answer down on his newspaper, then looks back at you with gratitude. "Yes," he continues, "your friend was here, with young Tom. Tom's here actually, perhaps she's still around. TOM!"

A young man emerges from the kitchen, drying his hands on his apron. You have to admit, he's surprisingly handsome for a place like Bradfell.

"That knight you had draped over you last night, she still here?" asks Oswald.

"Naw," says Tom, "we went for a walk to Sophia Park but then she fell asleep on the grass and I couldn't wake her up, so I just came home."

"Wait a sec," a voice suddenly growls from over your shoulder. It's Gwendolyn. "You just told them where she is, didn't you?" Tom nods, sheepishly, and Gwendolyn turns to Oswald. "Did they buy you a drink?"

"No," answers Oswald, his eyebrows turning downward defensively.

"You could have at least got them to buy us a round of drinks," Gwendolyn says, her voice rising in volume.

Oswald increases the volume of his voice to match. "But they got me the answer!"

"I don't care!" Gwendolyn shouts, slamming the table with her fist. Oswald rises from his seat and starts to shout into Gwendolyn's face, causing her to pick up a chair and fling it across the room.

You quickly back out of the tavern as the sounds of carnage increase behind you, and emerge into the colour of the crossroads.

Record the codeword *Stryver* and turn to **74**.

56

If you have the codeword *Defarge*, turn immediately to **398**.

If not, turn to **348**.

57 ☐

If the box above is ticked, turn immediately to **123**.

If not, put a tick in it now and turn to **69**.

58 ☐

If you have the codeword *Pross* and the box above is not ticked, put a tick in it now and turn to **392**.

If you do not have the codeword *Pross*, or if the box above is already ticked, turn to **270**.

59

You explain about the conversation you had with Orm, and the woman's face immediately softens.

"Oh, lovely! Look, I'm sorry to break it to you but that was a little test the sarge came up with. You know, you never can tell when an out-of-towner's going to stab you in the back. Thanks for letting us know, but he's actually an undercover BLEED officer. He's one of us. You're alright, do you know that? Hey: enjoy the city."

Record the codeword *Barsad*.

Ask to speak to Brannick   Turn to **335**

Ask for information or
equipment   Turn to **378**
Leave the building   Turn to **145**

60

If you have the codeword *Cly*, turn immediately
to **50**.

If not, turn to **255**.

61

"Manfred?" he replies, "Yes, yes, he's in here quite
often. Quite a character, eh? He was in here last
night actually."

If you have the codeword *Theophile*, turn to
112.

If not, but if you have the codeword *Foulon*,
turn to **374**. If you have neither, turn to **78**.

62

The smells of stale ale and sounds of
conversation drift out from the Fuming Fig as
you pass, and you almost fail to notice an
elaborate gate to your right, welcoming you into
Sophia Park. You can enter through the gate
(turn to **34**), or continue down the road (turn to
130).

63

"Ah, I'm afraid I don't have any necklaces. I did have one a bit ago from an eccentric fellah who lives over on Pride Place, but he came and bought it back. No idea why. If you want one, your best bet is to enter a game of Privy down the Fuming Fig, the prize for that is traditionally a necklace of some sort. It's meant to protect you from the pixies, some say."

What will you ask for now?

A set of lockpicks	Turn to **349**
A weapon	Turn to **91**
Sell something	Turn to **132**
Leave	Turn to **95**

64

The bold colours down Cobalt Lane are quite shocking, although your eyes quickly adapt, allowing you to notice the intricately sculpted wall of the Shrine of the Trickle of Wisdom to your left.

As you proceed down the road, carved drops of water turn into splashes, and then a great tidal wave that carries you to a crossroads (turn to **74**).

65

This corner of Wall Street is particularly dark.
The road is narrow and the workshops that make
up most of the estate to the north and east
generate more mechanical noise than you've ever
wanted to hear.

A narrow street bearing the optimistic name
of Afterlife Alley leads off to the north-east here,
and a large butcher's shop on the eastern wall
bearing a sign saying "Hobson's" catches your eye

as a place to pick up a pie to keep your strength up.

Opposite the butcher, a small group of locals in some sort of deep conversation look up at you as you arrive, but show no signs of wanting to converse.

Into the butcher	Turn to **164**
Clockwise: Wall Street	Turn to **313**
Anti-clockwise: Wall Street	Turn to **71**
North-east: Afterlife Alley	Turn to **317**

66

The moment you point out the cleaver, Hugnym leaps up in recognition. "Yes! That was it!" he cries. "Excellent. Why would Keegan have had a cleaver?"

He steps forward and picks it up, turning it in his hands. "And what's this?" he says, suddenly jerking the blade round to show you the handle. "Ah! I cut myself!" He sticks his finger in his mouth and tries to keep talking to you, so filled with excitement he can't keep it in. "Fee the inifoo on it?" You look and see the initials *HT* carved inexpertly into the handle. "Vatoo be Hobfon Kuckeck, ve bukfer. Ow."

Just about drawing the reasonable conclusion that the cleaver is owned by the butcher, you suggest that while Hugnym gets his finger taken care of, you go and speak to this Hobfon Kuckek, or whatever his name is.

When you enter the butcher's, add 50 to the section number to confront the proprietor about why their cleaver ended up at the scene of a murder.

When you are ready, you leave the crime scene (turn to 38).

67

They've got a headstart, but your fitness easily matches their natural speed and each time they duck into an alley you notice you're gaining ground.

They must have noticed that too, and ahead you notice them ducking into a doorway, slamming it behind them.

Will you plough straight into the door, your weapon out (turn to 250), or will you approach cautiously in case they have backup (turn to 94)?

68

You react with the best speed you can, throwing your fist out at his face for his face to run into it. He is faster though, ducking under your outstretched arm and wrapping his arms around you, his tiny fists clanging against your armour.

"Take a punch, tin man!" he yells.

Will you use your strength to push him away and dive on top of him (turn to 243) or swing your leg round to take his legs out from under him (turn to 106)?

69

You suddenly feel as if you're having a heart attack; an irritating vibration makes you clasp your hands against your chest, where they alight on the pendant you won in the game of Privy. It's shuddering as if about to explode and glowing an unnatural green colour.

As you look at it, wondering whether to hurl it away or clutch on for dear life, the shuddering stops, as if nothing had ever happened. You glance around you in case something affected it, but see nothing out of the ordinary, apart from a few crowds of pixies going about their daily duties.

Shrugging your shoulders, you take in the point you've reached: a T-junction, which also provides access to one of the city's more hidden parks.

North-west: Brown Alley	Turn to **321**
South-west: Freedom Lane	Turn to **138**
South-east: into Four Belly Gardens	Turn to **89**
North-east: Freedom Lane	Turn to **369**

70

As you begin to make your way down the hill, a piece of paper fluttering across your path catches your eye, and you step on it to take a look.

Œstrakkaltir

They're onto you. Flee, friend, flee!

Wandering who this Eestrakkaltir might be, and why "they" might be after them, you continue until you reach another junction (turn to **318**).

71
The people in this part of Bradfell are particularly filthy, even by this blasted city's standards, and as the road remains narrow you find yourself avoiding them as much as possible. One of them sneezes close to you, and it's all you can do not to curse them out loud.

Thankfully, it widens ahead as you reach Gait Gate (turn to **344**).

72 ☐
If the box above is ticked, turn immediately to **148**.

If not, put a tick in it now and turn to **221**.

73
No sooner have you said that you'll fight her, you see her balled fist swipes across her body at you, knuckle duster in hand.

Will you duck underneath the punch (turn to **211**) or lean away from it (turn to **368**)?

74

You have arrived at a bright and colourful junction and look up to see a shimmering pattern of shapes of light, dancing in the air as if by magic.

Perhaps it *is* magic.

Or perhaps it's just the rain.

In any case, they spell out to you that you have reached the Shaded Crossroads, from which each street bears its own colour scheme, making the Temple District visually quite distinct from the rest of the city.

Memorial Lane, with its deep blacks and greys, as if stepping into a supernatural shadow, leads north between two notable buildings: the Phoenix and Pheasant on its right, and the Shrine of the Trickle of Wisdom on its left. Directly opposite it lies Brown Alley, curving around to the left behind a large sign simply bearing the word "*WARNING!*", every building along which bears another surprising interpretation of the colour brown. Cobalt Lane, in blues and greens, leads west from here, curving around to the south-west ahead, while Golden Pathway in oranges and yellows leaves here to the east.

Into the Phoenix and Pheasant   Turn to **295**
Into The Shrine of the Trickle
of Wisdom   Turn to **314**
North: Memorial Lane   Turn to **179**
East: Golden Pathway   Turn to **31**
South: Brown Alley   Turn to **263**

75

You approach the man, whose hands drop limply to his sides, his expression rapidly becoming one of relief.

"Oh, thank goodness," he breathes at you, his voice raspy. "I'm about to die of thirst, and some witch cast a spell meaning I can't leave this blessed bench until I've had some water. Can you help?"

If you are carrying some water, you will know how to offer some to him; follow those instructions now if you'd like to.

If not, he understands, but asks that if you find him some and return with it, he'd be able to reward you.

What will you do now?

Stroll around the park	Turn to **129**
Leave: Freedom Lane	Turn to **167**
Leave: Brad Plaza	Turn to **242**

76

You instinctively turn from the boggarts and sprint down the hill, hearing over your shoulder that they have given chase.

As Wall Street approaches, you have to make a snap decision; will you turn left (turn to **9**) or right (turn to **273**)?

77

"Troll!" he exclaims. "Yes, that would make sense! Thank you!"

The fire quickly dies down, and within a few minutes has cooled sufficiently, allowing him to gently drop the device in his hand, extract his arm, and retrieve the instructions to release you all.

"Excellent," he says, leading you back into the shop. "So, what would you like to buy?"

You are stunned into silence for a moment.

"Hang on," Sir Engelard steps in, "didn't we just rescue you? Surely a reward is in order?"

Now it's the shopkeeper's turn to look stumped. "Well," he begins, and then stops himself. "I tell you what, I'll give you a discount. Five per cent off anything worth more than a Sophia."

Sir Tostig is already marching out of the shop. "We don't carry money," he explains.

"Oh, right," replies the shopkeeper. "Well, thank you for coming! Goodbye!"

Realising quickly that you're wasting your time here, you follow Sir Tostig and leave (turn to **80**).

78

"In fact, he was getting very friendly with one of you lot! Always nice to welcome one of the Protectors, I thought, but I hadn't counted on it being – oh, I forget her name now – you know, the grumpy one. With the beard. Julia! That's it, Sir Julia. Wow, she can drink anyone under the table, can't she? In fact, I think at one point they were drinking under the table. Oh, excuse me."

He follows the call of duty to help his staff change an ale barrel, leaving you alone at the bar. It appears that finding Sir Julia is even more important than you thought it would be, you're going to have to prioritise finding her now.

Record the codeword *Gabelle* before deciding what to do next.

Join the drinkers	Turn to **397**
Play a round of Privy	Turn to **176**
Leave: Dragontoothache Passage	Turn to **234**
Leave: Pride Pass	Turn to **222**

79

"Ah, welcome," a gravelly voice harshly says as you walk in through the door and close out the elements behind you. The owner of the voice, presumably Olfric, is a dwarf with a monobrow and a tricorn hat that he seems to be wearing back-to-front.

"Let me tell you," he starts to say without being invited to, "it's nice to have someone of your calibre in here for a change. The number of people I get in here that just come begging for me to take advantage of them is criminal. Did you know Bradfell has more bankrupt people than any other town within 50 miles? And most of them have their final transaction right here! Anyway, enough about me. what are you here for?"

How will you reply?

Sell something	Turn to **132**
Buy something specific	Turn to **203**
Just browse	Turn to **235**

80

You wade through a dense press of people who seem deep in debate about something, although when you ask a local the only answer you get is a meaningless phrase, accompanied by a chuckle that indicates you've unwittingly stepped into an in-joke: "That troll's up to his usual tricks again!"

You try to ignore the crowd as you take in the statue they must be talking about, that of a giant troll, wielding a traditional club in one hand and what looks like a delicate paintbrush in the other.

It is from this statue that this gate, Troll Gate, takes its name, and a Gates Carriage is boarding passengers as you arrive. A shop behind the statue bears the title "Troll Trinkets", and Clover Row offers a route into the centre of the city from here.

Into Troll Trinkets	Turn to **162**
Clockwise: Wall Street	Turn to **354**
Anti-clockwise: Wall Street	Turn to **13**
West: Clover Row	Turn to **178**
Onto the Gates Carriage	Turn to **10**

81

This narrow lane must be one of the least well-kept in the city but looks like one of the best-used, judging by the amount of filth, discarded items and broken glass that line its edges. A large door to your right presumably provides intolerable actors access backstage and so you hurry past it until it meets Long Lane ahead (turn to **161**).

82

You don't have to wait long before a quite delicious meal is served to you, far better than the fare you were offered last evening.

As you're eating, a young man comes and sits at your table and starts talking to you with some gibberish you can't make any sense of.

"I have heard that the dwarves are restless at this time of year," he says, carefully annunciating every word. He looks at you expectantly. How will you respond?

"That's probably because they're eternally grumpy."	Turn to **142**
"Yes, I plan to spend next month at the beach."	Turn to **227**
"The elves have started moving west."	Turn to **261**
"What are you talking about, you silly little man?"	Turn to **254**

83

The barman is friendly enough, and it doesn't take long to get him talking openly about the city.

"Oh, there's always plenty going on here you know," he says. "I'm sure Portsrood has its fair share of incidents in the court, but Bradfell has a certain...*shay mons prang*, if you catch my drift." He winks at you, leaving you wondering what he just said. "The latest I heard was of a secret passage at the bottom of Tortoise Walk, which takes you straight into the slums. If anyone's been causing trouble in the city, you can bet it'll be coming from there."

When you reach the bottom of Tortoise Walk, if you would like to search for a secret passage, multiply the section you are in by two and turn to this new section.

Greet the old man	Turn to **300**
Leave the Eager Griffon	Turn to **98**

84

The sounds of the city wafting around you and the sun beating on your back, you stride along the road until you reach another junction (turn to **184**).

85

The level walk along this road feeling distinctly different from the hill, you have a moment of minor appreciation as you march along it. That is, until you overhear a couple of locals in their painful accent, knocking you back to a state of frustration that you're still here. Mumbling to yourself, you continue until you reach another junction (turn to **184**).

86

You've only taken one step when the door behind you abruptly closes, leaving you in darkness. You scrabble around for a moment, looking for a way to get out, but there's nothing obvious.

You panic for a moment but shrug it off – maybe you can source a torch from the slum and return when you can see better.

Groping forwards in the dark, you descend a short flight of steps and walk forwards a few paces until the passageway ends in a solid wall. You feel around on every side, but there's no way out. Retracing your steps, tapping the walls as you go, you end up accepting that this tunnel has unfortunately become your tomb.

87

You make your way back through the hole in the fence and round to the back door, easily entering the same way you did last time.

This time, however, you quickly discover you are not alone. BLEED officers step behind you, and none other than Brannick steps out of the shadows.

"You have no good reason to be in here," he says. "We trusted the Protectors to work with us, and you have betrayed that trust. I have no option other than to arrest you, and I think it's a fair prediction that the trade deal will be called off as a result. Best of luck."

He turns to the other officers surrounding you. "Into the cells!" he says, and you are unceremoniously dragged away, the shame of your bad decision-making overshadowing you like a dark cloud as you conclude that you will never be able to return home again.

88

The gaudiness of the theatre on your right seems to spill over into the rest of this narrow street, and you imagine it is full of theatregoers when a show is being performed.

As you continue, a kerfuffle ahead attracts your attention, and the crowd ahead suddenly disperses, running right at you. You prepare yourself for battle but are helpless to stop the locals bustling you to the side, and just in time. One of the rare nobles who calls Bradfell home must have fallen off their chariot, and the two horses leading it are running down the street with no driver to control them!

Calmly, you observe the driverless chariot continue past you; you shrug your shoulders, and

carry on. At the end of the large building, you reach a junction (turn to **145**).

89

Four Belly Gardens is one of the smaller parks in the city but you find it nice enough, in that for a moment or two you might be able to convince yourself that you're no longer in Bradfell.

A handful of roughly carved wooden benches are strewn around the space. Most are empty, but one is playing host to a bearded man in a pork pie hat, who seems to be trying to get your attention by waving his hands around.

Approach the man	Turn to **75**
Stroll around the park	Turn to **129**
Leave: Freedom Lane	Turn to **167**
Leave: Brad Plaza	Turn to **270**

90

The Eager Griffon is a disconcertingly bright tavern, its walls covered with useless trinkets gathered from every corner of the civilised world. You can't help yourself instinctively bowing your head at a portrait of Queen Sophia, but immediately stop yourself when you notice it has been placed next to an image of the corrupt Lord Zazzarel, astride a great lizard and wearing the rag that passes for a crown in his false kingdom of Mesrelot.

Turning away from the pictures, you accidentally meet the eyes of an old, balding man, casually leaning against the bar. He raises a glass to you and takes a sip, without moving his eyes from you. Aside from him, the only other people in here are the barman, and a shady-looking character smoking a thin pipe in the corner, clearly trying to avoid your gaze.

Speak to the barman	Turn to **370**
Greet the old man	Turn to **300**
Approach the shady character	Turn to **364**
Leave the Eager Griffon	Turn to **98**

91

He quickly glances around when you ask for a weapon, before narrowing his eyes and staring straight at you.

"Alright," he says, his voice lowered to a gruff whisper, "I don't normally do this for strangers, but you look like someone with a particular set of needs, and I do like to be of service. I have something in the back room, if you'd like to see it?"

Will you go with him to see whatever he has in the back room (turn to **166**), or say you'll leave it for now (turn to **302**)?

92

You feel a slight heat emerging on your brow and lift your hand involuntarily to find out what it is, but the source of the warmth remains a mystery. As you are touching your hand against your forehead, a pretty young lady with dark skin and a prominent tattoo creeping up the side of her face approaches.

"Ah, there you are," she says confidently. "You look strong and brave, that's good. The last time a victor came this way he was – well, never mind. Come on then, this way."

She starts to wander off without looking back. Will you go with her (turn to **260**), or not (turn to **256**)?

93

Leaving the garish teals of Cobalt Lane behind you, it's only a few buildings before the bright whites of a crossroad ahead take over your visual senses.

You notice a physician located here, with the trust-building and brave name of Bottomley Pratt plastered over its window.

You can visit the physician if you wish (turn to **127**), or continue to the south-east (turn to **213**).

94

Carefully opening the door, you gingerly step inside, looking around you. Confusingly, the place looks deserted, when suddenly a shadow dropping on you from above causes you to spin around.

Before you are able to take in what's happening, a heavy object collides with your head and you fall to the floor, unconscious.

Turn to **11**.

95

The rain falling all around you seems to carry a golden sheen, as the light reflecting off the paving stones to the west bounces across the sheets of water. There is no cover here and so you are keen to move on from here as quickly as possible, although a shop entrance under a sign declaring it to provide access to "Olfric's Pawnne Shoppe" offers temporary respite from the storm.

Into Olfric's Pawnne Shoppe	Turn to **79**
North: Tortoise Walk	Turn to **290**
East: Magicians Alley	Turn to **307**
West: Golden Pathway	Turn to **264**

96

"Did you hear that this year's joust was cancelled?" he murmurs at you, his moustache adding an odd white noise to accompany his words.

You admit that you hadn't heard; knights of a lower order may keep up-to-date on these regional contests, but the sporting calendar of an out-of-the-way place like Bradfell isn't the sort of thing you have time for.

"Well," he continues unperturbed, "word is, Lady Lloyd wasn't happy about it. Following her exile, the joust has been the only day she's been allowed back into the city, so that's been delayed. Apparently, she refuses to have her hair cut anywhere other than Bradfell, and so it's grown so long she was mistaken for a tree! Can you believe it?"

Judging by the haircut worn by the man currently taking up your vision, you have no difficulty imagining someone choosing to stoop lower looking more like flora than human.

You smile and move on. Will you leave onto Faraway Road (turn to **320**) or Long Lane (turn to **175**)?

97

You are at Gait Gate, set into the city wall at the northernmost point of the slums that extend around the south-west outer edge of the city.

The impressive Faraway Road leads up the hill to the east of here, while Wall Street extends along the city walls in both directions, around which the Gates Carriage regularly offers faster travel to each of the city gates.

There is also a rather grand entrance to Sophia Park here, the sight of which causes your chest to swell with pride as you remember the Queen, back in your beloved Portsrood.

Clockwise: Wall Street	Turn to **155**
Anti-clockwise: Wall Street	Turn to **105**

East: Faraway Road	Turn to **292**
South-east: into Sophia Park	Turn to **34**
Onto the Gates Carriage	Turn to **10**

98

You are immediately outside the Eager Griffon, the tavern best known for enabling punters to meet travelling bards after their performances in Bradfell Theatre. Thankfully, no shows are currently on and so you run no risk of having to meet any.

The optimistically titled Laughing Walk leads north from here, while Dragontoothache Passage stretches up and down the hill.

Into the Eager Griffon	Turn to **5**
North: Laughing Walk	Turn to **223**
East: Dragontoothache Passage	Turn to **101**
South-west: Dragontoothache Passage	Turn to **117**

99

The grim weather continues, and you can't help feeling positive about the promise of sitting under the closed roof of a Gates Carriage that you see up ahead at Lonely Gate.

Your feet slosh through the awful rain as you arrive (turn to **108**).

Sophia Park is a big place to search, but it's the only place you know to look for Sir Julia and so you begin to look around.

The park is full of people out walking, talking, and relaxing, but the sight of a mound of shiny metal sticking out from behind a bush draws your attention before too long, and it turns out to be her.

Using all your strength, you tug at her feet until she's out in the open, her beard picking up twigs as you go. Her heavy breathing puts any concerns about her having died to rest, although she is known for being a heavy sleeper.

Do you have some water to splash over her? If so, follow the instructions you were given when you obtained it.

If not, you are left with no other option than to try to slap her awake (turn to **241**).

The experimental clothing of those that surround you as you continue along the road is getting close to offending you. You catch yourself thinking that whoever invented the idea of self-expression needs to take a long, hard look at themselves.

You quickly conclude that they would probably sabotage even that, by narcissistically appreciating the act of self reflection.

Muttering, you arrive at another junction (turn to 145).

102

All of a sudden, the air around you stills. Some powerful magic is at play, and you don't like the tingling feel of it against your skin. If only Lord Tostig were here.

You grab hold of your weapon in readiness for whatever threat is about to lay hold of you, but a light tap on the back of your helmet causes you to turn around.

There's no-one there.

Holding your weapon in front of you and turning slowly, your peripheral vision on full alert, you begin to feel very uneasy, when another tap on the back of your helmet rings around you, and this time you spin on the spot, catching a glimpse of a bright light trying to dart out of your field of vision.

You continue to spin, and grab out at the moving thing, skilfully clutching it in your hand.

You identify it quickly as a dark pixie, a race you thought had been eliminated due to the danger they pose to humans. You remember learning once that they like to send one of their own to disorient a victim before using magic to cause their internal organs to spontaneously stop operating.

Looking up from the dark pixie in your hand, you suddenly find that you're unsure whereabouts you are. A moment ago, you could have sworn you were in Bradfell.

Then, a flash fills your vision, bringing with it a sudden pain while-

103

You clamber across people getting in your way, knocking them down as you go, and finally get to a point where you can leap at the fleeing man, tackling him to the ground.

You don't have to wait any time before a handful of BLEED officers arrive, who put him under arrest and lead you up the hill to the City Hall (turn to **400**).

104

Wall Street begins to narrow as it continually turns to the right, taking you into Artificers' Quarter. The blue smoke emerging from the houses along the right-hand wall seems to sit on the road ahead of you, waiting to trick you with a sudden burst of activity, although none transpires.

Ahead, the road bends around to the left at the entrance to a narrow alley, and you approach (turn to **65**).

105

After some time walking, the road bends around to the left and then back to the right. The sounds of birds accompanied by the odd shout that reach you from the other side of the houses to your left must come from Sophia Park.

Before too long, you have reached a T-junction (turn to **130**).

106

He nimbly jumps over your attempt to take him down, laughing as he does so.

"Are you serious?" he yells, landing on your feet and grabbing hold of your torso. You feel his fingers at the edges of your breastplate but that sensation turns quickly into pain as a hidden blade pierces your skin and begins worming its way through your ribcage.

The unsettling smiling face of your killer accompanies the echoing sounds of bloodthirsty cheers as you pass from life to death.

107

The thing about punching upwards with people who don't carry around much weight is the surprise that's consistently delivered by the trajectory taken by the body. His neck snapping backwards, you manage to launch his body up into the air and he defies gravity for a moment before landing on the floor in a dishevelled heap.

"Good work," the man from outside says, clapping as he closes the distance to you. "I knew you'd fit right in. Oh, hold still a moment." He holds his hand towards you, palm facing outwards, and mutters something: *"Rastiad endoe sayeltiad ponaytos.* That'll do it. You now carry a magic mark so all will know you've been victorious here. Well, all who matter, anyway."

Satisfied that you've done what you needed to, you return up the stairs and walk outside.

Record the codeword *Alexandre* and turn to **21**.

108

You quickly duck into an alcove that sits alongside Lonely Gate and take stock of your surroundings while the rain continues to pour. Wall Street continues in both directions along the city walls, and three other streets lead away from this point.

Freedom Lane leads off directly in front of the gate to the south-west, climbing a slight gradient past a permanent street sign simply bearing the word *WARNING.* A narrower road, Magicians Alley, offers a route directly to the west, while Danger Alley climbs a steeper hill to the south, immediately leaping around to the right.

Clockwise: Wall Street	Turn to **337**
Anti-clockwise: Wall Street	Turn to **389**
South: Danger Alley	Turn to **189**
South-west: Freedom Lane	Turn to **380**

West: Magicians Alley   Turn to **282**

Onto the Gates Carriage   Turn to **10**

109

You are in the heart of the residential district most densely populated by young families here, and the shrieks of children on every side continually remind you of that fact. Wall Street sits in the shadow of the hill of Bradfell at this point, at the base of a road leading up it to the north-east, bearing the name Resolution Hill.

The corner of the block here boasts a cheery-looking building, containing nine doors on three levels, with stairs criss-crossing one another to allow access. Each of the doors bears a symbol but you can't make any sense of them. There's one that looks like a misshapen diamond, another that looks like a clod of earth, and another that looks like an orange.

Directly opposite it, a violin player seems to be trying to entertain a family you can only conclude must be his own; no-one would stand for that racket if they didn't have to.

Clockwise: Wall Street	Turn to **296**
Anti-clockwise: Wall Street	Turn to **385**
North: Resolution Hill	Turn to **208**

110

The herb garden is a well-tended series of bushes in the rear courtyard of the Husband's House. You wander up and down the oddly-shaped pathways, noticing that they bend and twist around one another, forming the shape of a – well, you wouldn't like to say. One of the wives, reclining on a bench in the corner, gives you a brief tour without standing or looking up once.

"We grow all manner of herbs here. Flavouring, seasoning – those are two different sciences, did you know? – medicines, psychedelics, poisons...would you like to take some with you?"

The majority of the plants are various shades of green, with different-shaped leaves and intoxicating scents, although a few are much more visually distinctive, with colours and shapes that make the whole thing a dangerously rich multisensory experience.

Ask to take some	Turn to **20**
Speak to Husband Graham	Turn to **275**
Get a blessing from a wife	Turn to **303**
Leave into Black Dragon Grounds	Turn to **47**
Leave onto Wall Street	Turn to **194**

111

The shimmering blues and greens of Cobalt Lane accompany you as you leave the Shaded Crossroads behind. This is a busy road, as crowds move between the Temple District and Long Lane, and you have to take particular care to not touch any of the rabble in case they are carrying something contagious, like poverty for example.

Before too long, you arrive at Long Lane (turn to **175**).

112

"In fact, wasn't he in here with you?" He gestures at Sir Julia. "Oh, excuse me." He follows the call of duty to help his staff change an ale barrel, leaving you alone at the bar.

Sir Julia looks stunned for a moment, and then her eyes widen.

"Oh yeeessss," she says, carefully considering her next words. "Now that you mention it, it does look a bit familiar in here. Yes, he was talking about making some money or some such nonsense. It all sounded a bit fishy now I remember. We even went back to his place for a bit. Hey! Wouldn't it be a good idea to find it? If only I could remember where it was. Do you know, I'm sure I'll know it when I see it. It was right by a city gate that had a great big sculpture above it in the shape of two entwined people. Shall we head out?" She starts marching towards the exit, perhaps wanting to avoid you discovering any more of her antics from the previous night.

When you reach the location at which you think Manfred's house sits, add 50 to the section number and turn to this new section.

Leave north-east:
Dragontoothache Passage   Turn to **234**
Leave south-east: Pride Pass   Turn to **222**

113

You find Edgar's house without too much difficulty, in spite of the rain cascading down around you, and knock hard on the door.

It opens a crack, and his face emerges.

"Did you do it?" he asks, and you force your way inside and out of the rain, causing him to panic for a moment about the water on his floor before he begins to panic about the potential consequences of offending you.

You tell him about the children you met, and his face melts with empathy.

"Yes, of course. We must help them, absolutely. We'll surely be able to force the Council subtly to discover the deed and let us in. Listen. Let me get my papers ready, and we can head over there together. Meet me at Gait Gate in twenty minutes, and organise everything. We're going to help those poor children."

Record the codeword *Launay*.

Beginning to get frustrated by the wild goose chase Edgar has sent you on so far, you leave his house and step back into the rain (turn to **108**).

114

The Eager Griffon is a disconcertingly bright tavern, its walls covered with useless trinkets gathered from every corner of the civilised world. You can't help yourself instinctively bowing your head at a portrait of Queen Sophia, but immediately stop yourself when you notice it has been placed next to an image of the corrupt Lord Zazzarel, astride a great lizard and wearing the rag that passes for a crown in his false kingdom of Mesrelot.

Turning away from the pictures, you accidentally meet the eyes of an old, balding man, casually leaning against the bar. He raises a

80

glass to you and takes a sip, without moving his eyes from you. Aside from him, the only other people in here are the barman.

Speak to the barman	Turn to **83**
Greet the old man	Turn to **300**
Leave the Eager Griffon	Turn to **98**

115

If you have codeword *Gaspard*, turn immediately to **386**. If not, read on.

The Blessed House of the Husband of Countless Wives and Sagas of Courageous Acts With Said Wives is a large, multi-storey, intricate building, full of corridors and small rooms. The walls and furniture are all pristine, and the smell of fresh food wafts through every space you explore here.

This is the spiritual and physical home of Husband Graham, along with his many wives, of which there are dozens. All dressed in white robes, their primary activity seems to be to talk to one another, while the brown-robed servants, almost all of whom are suspiciously good-looking men, hurry around doing the chores.

Speak to Husband Graham	Turn to **275**
Get a blessing from a wife	Turn to **303**
Visit the herb garden	Turn to **110**
Leave into Black Dragon Grounds	Turn to **47**
Leave onto Wall Street	Turn to **194**

116

You are standing at the top of the Clover Row steps that lead down to a large statue in front of a city gate in the distance. Clover Row itself continues away from the steps to your west, while The Saunter, a long, road in the shadow of the City Hall, leads north from here, bending around to the north-east in the distance.

As you are considering where to head next, a local treads on your foot. You are about to berate him when he trips and begins to steadily fall down the steps to the east. When he eventually reaches the bottom, he simply stands, brushes himself down and keeps on walking.

North: The Saunter	Turn to **288**
East: Clover Row	Turn to **265**
West: Clover Row	Turn to **331**

117

You trip over the moment you decide to start walking, the clanging sound of your armour on the cobblestones reverberating against the buildings as if someone had just composed a particularly tuneless motif for percussion. As you angrily stand yourself and stomp off again, you can almost hear the creativity of those behind you being kicked into gear, and you grimace as you imagine a new concoction emerging in a couple of months' time, dedicated to you.

You pass a few nondescript buildings, and arrive at another junction (turn to **234**).

118

Bradfell Theatre rising up to your left, the detritus from past performances is pasted all along the wall. You find yourself casually reading the posters, and can't help noticing a likeness of a younger version of yourself, promoting a tour that the Protectors took through Bradfell several years ago. You have no memory of it, and probably for good reason.

Leaving the poster behind, you walk to the end of the theatre and the edge of Brad Plaza (turn to **29**).

119

You share with the group the stream of clues you've followed, and that it led you to Husband Graham. Everyone gathered round looks shocked, and stares at him expectantly.

With a calm air, he says, "Well, there must be some sort of explanation, mustn't there? Wait a minute," he sniffs the air, "what's that smell?"

He moves closer to you and takes a deep breath. "Can anyone else smell that?"

A couple of others agree with him, and within a few moments your pouch has been opened and Brannick is looking at you in disbelieving shock and fury.

"Why are you carrying around poisonous herbs?" he demands, and then draws his own conclusion. "You poisoned Manfred!"

You can't stop the chain of events that then takes place, beginning with your arrest and leading to all chance of a trade deal between Bradfell and Portsrood being dashed.

This has been a less than successful business trip.

120

You try to move along the road but the crowds here become denser than you would like, threatening you at every point with having to touch the common folk. You begin to mutter to yourself in irritation.

Finally, the crowds shift around you and you are presented with enough space to make your way forward until you reach a crossroads (turn to **38**).

121

You don't stop running and barely notice as rain begins to fall around you, the buildings on your left and the city wall on your right both blurring until you finally pause for a moment. Risking a glance behind you, you are grateful to realise that you seem to have lost your pursuer.

Now drenched, you heart pounding and feeling overwhelmed with confusion at what just happened, you look up to get your bearings (turn to **183**).

122

The exotic smells of Velveteen Walk cloak you, and you subconsciously hold your breath to protect yourself from the pretention of it all. If you were from Bradfell, perhaps you'd want to spend your time pretending you were from somewhere else, but can't they do it from the discomfort of their own homes?

The gaudy colours of Brad Plaza up ahead don't please your eyes much more than the smells of incense pleased your nostrils, but at least you feel like there's less pretence here (turn to **29**).

123

You have reached the midway point of Freedom Lane, where it meets Brown Alley and also provides access to one of the city's lesser-known parks.

South-west: Freedom Lane	Turn to **138**
North-east: Freedom Lane	Turn to **369**
North-west: Brown Alley	Turn to **321**
South-east: into Four Belly Gardens	Turn to **89**

124

A guard house sits halfway along the city wall in the stretch you are walking down, and the houses opposite are notable for having no entrances leading onto Wall Street itself, opting instead for tiny passages that presumably lead to side entrances. You wonder whether these two are linked as you proceed along the road, reaching another T-junction (turn to 357).

125

This road must be home to some of Bradfell's bothersome creative types; you remember that it's known for producing a high volume of poor-quality bards and jesters. A juggler seems to be trying to attract your attention, and so you ignore him and hurry onward (turn to 98).

126

You shout at the top of your lungs, and a woman immediately in front of you suddenly turns, holding her hands to her ears, a furious expression on her face.

"That's not Husband Graham, you idiot! Now keep your voice down."

Disappointed and embarrassed, you stop moving, and then an arm alights on your shoulder. It's one of the BLEED officers, breathing heavily from having chased after you.

"Brannick got him."

You follow the officer to the City Hall, where Brannick is waiting with the now apprehended Husband Graham (turn to 400).

127

The physician's office looks grand from the outside, and a young lady is leaving through its wide open door as you approach. Once you're inside, however, the scene changes somewhat.

Rather than an extravagant space as you would have assumed, the interior is quite small and spartan. A single desk with a pair of chairs sits off to one side, faced by a small bench for patients to wait on. A man with a great handlebar moustache in a white gown you assume must be Bottomley Pratt is deep in conversation with a short lady clutching a bunch of flowers, and he waves you over to the bench as you enter.

"Nothing to worry about," he is saying as you take your seat. "One quick kiss either side of the bed, and you'll be right as rain."

"Thank you," the lady says delicately, before handing over the flowers and leaving through the front door.

Pratt turns to you. "So, how can I help?"

If you have the codeword *Pross*, turn to **23**. If not, turn to **304**.

128

As you open the door and step into the shop, the sound of a horn hooting makes you physically jump with surprise.

"Wait just a sec!" comes a shout from a door set into the back wall, and so you take a moment to glance around.

"Trinkets" is a generous title for the items on display here. Useless pieces of junk and tat have been displayed around the shop, some precariously balanced on the edge of shelves and others delicately formed into pyramids to boast how many of them – unsurprisingly – remain unsold. As you step forward, a model of a dragon hanging from the ceiling bounces off your helmet, making a tinny ringing sound.

"Actually," comes the voice again, "would you mind awfully coming through and giving me a hand with this? I'm having a bit of trouble."

Unsure about whether you want to get yourself involved with whatever the shopkeeper is doing, you quickly consider leaving surreptitiously. Will you walk out (turn to **80**), or step through to the back room (turn to **146**)?

129

The park isn't very large, and within ten minutes or so you've wandered around the perimeter and taken in everything it has to see: trees, bushes, and a variety of grasses.

One large boulder catches your eye as it appears to have something carved into it. Getting closer, the cryptic message makes itself clear:

Rusty bars break easily.

Pondering its deeper meaning, you consider what to do next.

Approach the man	Turn to **75**
Leave onto Freedom Lane	Turn to **167**
Leave into Brad Plaza	Turn to **242**

130 ☐

If the box above is not ticked and you have the codeword *Solomon*, put a tick in it now and turn to **141**.

If the box above is already ticked, or if you do not have the codeword *Solomon*, turn to **197**.

131 ☐

If the box above is ticked, turn immediately to turn to **242**.

If not, put a tick in it now and turn to **329**.

132

When Olfric asks what you'd like to sell, you pause. Possessions are a rather foreign concept to you, as you have never had to buy anything before, and so Olfric steps in to help.

"How about your sword? It looks a bit beaten up, you could sell that one to me and get yourself a new one?"

It's at this point that you realise you would have no idea what a good price for a sword would be, and would have no use for the money in any case. You hurriedly change the topic.

| Buy something specific | Turn to **203** |
| Just browse | Turn to **235** |

133

The seemingly endless Wall Street continues to the north-west before bending ever so slightly towards the north, the building on your left an enormous hall, with dark, exposed beams of wood highlighting its structure from the outside.

The road ahead widens slightly at the point that a gate has been constructed into the city walls (turn to **80**).

134

If you have the codeword *Defarge*, turn immediately to **398**.

If not, turn to **125**.

135 ☐

If the box above is ticked, turn immediately to **249**.

If not, put a tick in it now and turn to **219**.

136

If you have the codeword *Jourdan*, turn immediately to **253**.

If not, turn to **262**.

137

The moment you start your descent you almost slip and your heart leaps in your chest; it is as if a leap forwards would plunge you a death-defying distance towards the ground below.

Without warning, a few spots of rain begin to appear on the cobbles and within a minute you are in a downpour, making the road the perfect place to slip and fall. Thinking that you will probably take an alternative route to the base of the hill next time you reach this point, you carefully make your way to the bottom (turn to **108**).

138

You climb the hill alone, the sight of the crowds on Long Lane ahead looking uninviting. You tell yourself that if you keep on moving, surely you'll find a way out of this hell sooner rather than later.

You are still muttering to yourself as you reach a junction at the top of the hill (turn to **38**).

139

Leaving the entrance to the Blessed House of the Husband of Countless Wives and Sagas of Courageous Acts with Said Wives behind you, you continue along the lengthy road known as Memorial Lane for quite some distance before you eventually arrive at a crossroads (turn to **74**).

140 ☐

If the box above is ticked, turn immediately to **87**.
If not, put a tick in it now, and turn to **60**.

141

As you arrive at a junction, two grubby little children run up to you, tears rolling down their faces, holding one another's hands. The younger one, a boy by the looks of things, can't stop rubbing his hands and nose with his clenched fist, while the slightly older one, a girl, looks up at you longingly.

"Oh, please help us!" she cries. She goes on to explain that they are brother and sister, and that they were taken away from their parents several months ago by a man called De-Sym. He was transporting them but they escaped into the city, and are now locked in, unable to return to their hometown of Cottage Bush to the south.

It occurs to you that if Edgar gets given access to the Portsrood Palace building, he may be able to help the children out. You tell the children to head straight there. Edgar said he lived just next to Lonely Gate, so you could go and find him. When you reach Lonely Gate, if you'd like to find Edgar, add 5 to the section number you are on and turn to this new section number.

When you are ready, turn to **197**.

142

The man looks disappointed.

"Oh," he says. "Yes, I suppose they are. Goodbye."

He walks away, leaving you confused, but grateful to be rid of him. You finish up, and leave the inn when you're ready (turn to **357**).

143

He clashes into you, his sweaty flesh landing squarely on your armour to leave greasy stains all over your breastplate.

"Boo!" he shouts into your face. "Fight me, you weakling!"

While this close to him you'll struggle to get an attack in. Will you suddenly duck down in an attempt to use his weight against him and tip him over you (turn to **217**), or will you viciously lift your knee up into his groin (turn to **196**)?

144

The junction you have just reached is shaped like a Y, at the centre of which is an unimaginative well. The buildings that grow up around you at this point look evil and smell like disgusting habits, and you shiver involuntarily.

Investigate the well	Turn to **210**
North-east: Shepherd Hill	Turn to **70**
South: Farewell Walk	Turn to **297**
North-west: Downwards Passage	Turn to **7**

145

You are at the point where Dragontoothache Passage meets Dreary Crescent, which surrounds the back of the theatre.

BLEED headquarters is located on the south point where the roads meet; you amuse yourself for a moment by wandering if you ought to report a crime against good form in the shape of this accursed city, and then think better of it.

Into BLEED headquarters   Turn to **326**
North: Dreary Crescent   Turn to **81**
East: Dreary Crescent   Turn to **118**
West: Dragontoothache Passage   Turn to **19**

146

The moment you step through, it's clear why he cried out in the manner in which he did. The wiry man, wearing a multicoloured waistcoat, his neat, triangular goatee beard looking as if it's trying to divert your attention to the centre of his chest, was perhaps fixing an undefinable contraption when he somehow passed the point of no return.

"Oh, thank you!" he says, his head turned at an awkward angle to greet you as his body cannot move away from the device. "I've got hold of it, but if I move it will drop."

You step deeper into the room, and Sir Tostig's hand on your forearm underlines the gravity of the situation that hit you as soon as you saw what the device contained.

A small fire has been lit at the bottom of a chute, above which several cylinders extend, presumably to allow for fuel to be funnelled in. The man's arm is fully contained within one of these cylinders, his hand holding onto an item that looks unforgivingly explosive, and larger than the cylinder, preventing him from removing it.

You have a look at the machine and, to cut a long story short, within a few minutes both you and your fellow knights are stuck inside the thing with him.

The only possible salvation for you will be to quench the fire, but the little man cheerily explains to you that it has been magically enchanted to be unquenchable.

"One of the perks, they said," he explains. "Not to worry though, I have the instructions on how to put it out. They're just up there on the shelf."

Of course, none of you can reach the shelf, and so you have no option other than to question why this eternally optimistic fool lit an unquenchable fire and then decided to hold a bomb directly above it.

"I tried to remember how," he continues, not at all apologetic – or even aware, apparently – that you are all in mortal peril, "but I keep getting the magic word wrong. I knew I wanted something I'd remember easily, and so I asked them to set it as something like statue, or gate, or Clover Row, but none of those seem to have worked. Any ideas?"

If you think you know what the magic word is, turn it into a number by turning each letter in the answer into a number following the pattern A=1, B=2, C=3, etc, and adding them all together. Turn to that section number, and you will know you have the right answer because it will be the first word in the section.

If you can't work out the answer, your fate is unfortunately marked out for you. Nobody else will come to the shop for the rest of the day, and after several hours of no food, drink and sleep, the annoying little shopkeeper will drop the bomb, taking you all with him into the afterlife.

147

The source of the light becomes apparent as soon as you reach the doorway: a flickering torch in a sconce is causing a chest full of gold and jewels to bounce the light around in mystifying ways.

You all break into a big grin, and Sir Engelard is the first to reach forward. You hear a sudden cry from above of "Don't touch tha-"

The explosion from the illusion trap experiment is greater than the apprentice wizard had planned for, but your sacrifice is not in vain. Your unplanned intervention in her final exams go on to be used as an example of good practice for decades to come, and the Engelard Effect enters the standard curriculum for wizards in training majoring in illusion magic.

148

The Duke of Vanhelm is much the same as it was before. The waitress gives you a welcoming nod as you enter, but doesn't offer you anything else to eat or drink and so you leave (turn to 357).

149

The sounds of the busy open space ahead of you give you plenty of notice that Travellers Place is your next destination, and the sight of Travellers Gate, which greeted you as you first arrived and therefore seems to promise a route back to Portsrood, gives you a nudge of homesickness that you weren't expecting.

You find yourself holding your breath as you reach the gate (turn to 204).

150

You pass over the water, and he gratefully takes a generous gulp before passing it back to you. Breathing deeply, he delicately tries to stand and is elated when he is able to leave the bench.

"Oh, thank you so much!" He pulls out a long pipe, leaning against a tree to light it before continuing. "Now, let me introduce myself properly to you. My name's Orm, and I'm a

174
nouembre

1620

99

carpenter. In fact, I carved these benches. But that's all in the past now...anyway, about your reward. I don't have anything on me right now to offer you, but I have the greatest chance to get some real loot if you give me a hand with something."

Will you tell him that the knowledge you've helped a fellow human is reward enough (turn to 186), or will you ask him to continue (turn to 291)?

151

"I heard the oddest thing the other day," he begins, his moustache waggling to add drama to what he's saying. "The new jester's school that everyone's been talking about the past few months, you know, the one off to the west in Castle Barayvanhelm, well, how much do you think it costs to qualify there?"

He looks at you expectantly, and you have to admit you have no idea. Not only is currency something you barely have to deal with, the idea of spending any time in a jester's school out of choice is so foreign to you that your mind simply refuses to engage with the question.

"Well, you'd think it's something, wouldn't you? But no, it isn't. It costs nothing to join, but you have to bring with you an original copy of a traditional poem that some local bandits have stolen. Can you believe it? Listen, I've heard that you need to cast some spells to get into the wizard's college. Seems a bit daft to me, that. Prove you can do something so I can teach you how to do it. Circular reasoning, that is. But at least it's connected. For the jester's school, you need to prove you're on a killing spree to get in. Hey! You ever wanted to be a jester?"

You admit you haven't, before backing off politely and hurriedly finding a way to get out. Will you leave onto Faraway Road (turn to **320**) or Long Lane (turn to **175**)?

152

Politicians Regret steadies your climb through a winding incline that rounds a variety of large town houses overlooking the city gate below. The people surrounding you as you climb betray the arrogant signs of privilege, although at least you're not running the risk of catching poverty from the rest of this infernal city.

Having traversed the zig-zagging road up the hill, you reach Politicians Court (turn to **2**).

153

Grateful to be turning your back on the character whose name is as ridiculous as his legacy, your first steps down the hill are so fast on the cobbles, you almost trip forwards.

A crossroads ahead looks like it is built around a bandstand of some sort, and you approach with curiosity (turn to **184**).

154

You climb up the steps and knock on the door with the not-quite-circular mark on it. A few moments later, the door creaks open to reveal a short man, his dirty white sleeves rolled up and a monocle dangling from his breast pocket.

After a brief interaction it turns out that he is the Green Teabag, and to your surprise he seems to be a competent forger. It takes him barely any time, and twenty minutes later you have in your hand the false copy of the deed, ready to plant in the fake Portsrood Palace drawer.

Record the codeword *Cly*.

When you are ready to leave, you step back outside (turn to **109**).

155

If you have the codeword *Defarge*, turn immediately to **398**.

If not, turn to **104**.

156

The houses that overlook the Fuming Fig form a tightly-packed terrace, behind which you can hear the screams of children playing. You keep an eye out for an alleyway that will grant you access, but none appears before you arrive at Dragontoothache Passage (turn to **234**).

157

A professional queueing system is in place to obtain a blessing, giving you a warm, fuzzy feeling inside. Regardless of what anyone might say about the despicable state of Bradfell culture, no-one can claim that they don't know how to queue.

When your turn arrives, you are welcomed into a comfortable, cosy booth with one of Husband Graham's wives to receive your blessing.

Unfortunately, the definition of the word "blessing" according to this place would appear to be different from any previous definition of it you've experienced. The "blessing" turns out to be a detailed and unnecessarily graphic story about an intimate experience the wife shared with Husband Graham recently.

When she's finished, you step out of the booth, bored, disgusted, and curious to investigate the extracurricular uses of a pestle and mortar.

What will you do next?

Speak to Husband Graham   Turn to **247**
Leave into Black Dragon Grounds Turn to **47**
Leave onto Wall Street   Turn to **194**

158

You are standing on Long Lane at the top of Faraway Road, which leads off to the south-west.

The bright white building of the Sanctuary of Humility causes a dark shadow to fall over most of the west of the city, and its monks with their pious expressions loiter around the front door, welcoming in visitors with scornful expressions.

South-east: Long Lane   Turn to **120**
South-west: Faraway Road   Turn to **190**
North-west: Long Lane   Turn to **350**
Into the Sanctuary of Humility   Turn to **26**

159

Almost as soon as you start up Thunder Slop, you find yourself instinctively wanting to move onto all fours as if scaling the side of a mountain. Now that you think about it, you'd probably be more comfortable on the side of a mountain, because at least you wouldn't be so close to the Bradfell riff-raff as you are here.

Ropes have been connected to the sides of the buildings up this road, and you grab hold of one to prevent yourself slipping and falling back down. It levels off somewhat as you reach a junction (turn to **185**).

160

Ahead of you, a half-dozen squat, hairy men with long, slender arms stumble out of the inn bearing the name the Fuming Fig. You instinctively hold your hand to your mouth to stop yourself being sick at the sight of these disgusting boggarts, and are surprised that no-one else seems to be reacting to them.

As one of them points at you and yells something in their simple language, the others turn towards and move in your direction, picking up speed.

You will have to respond to this threat; will you ready yourself to fight (turn to **266**), or turn and run (turn to **76**)?

161

You arrive at Preachers Corner and stop to get your bearings. Leading away from Brad Plaza to the north-west is Long Lane, which you understand reaches all the way to the city walls far off in the distance.

A narrow alleyway declaring itself as Dreary Crescent – a fitting title to almost any street here in Bradfell – does nothing to entice you behind the theatre to the south, but remains an option.

Into the City Hall	Turn to **358**
East: Slum Corner	Turn to **58**
South-east: Politicians Court	Turn to **2**
South: Travellers Court	Turn to **29**
South-west: Dreary Crescent	Turn to **44**
North-west: Long Lane	Turn to **181**

162 ❑

If the box above is ticked, turn immediately to **371**.

If not, put a tick in it now and turn to **128**.

163

The tankard is the classic pewter common across the region, and it has clearly seen better days. Intrigued as to what sort of ale Manfred had been drinking you smell it, and immediately recognise that something is off.

The floral fragrance – the sort of thing Bradfell types would probably infuriatingly describe as "hoppy" – is definitely that of acontro, a poisonous herb that is odourless most of the time, but once crushed takes on strange smell after a few hours.

If you find the place these herbs could have come from, multiply the section number you are in by three, and turn to this new section.

Investigate the body	Turn to **308**
Look out of the window	Turn to **287**
Investigate the crooked painting	Turn to **30**
Investigate the clothes	Turn to **360**
Leave	Turn to **226**

164

The butcher's is as uninspiring on the inside as it is on the outside. The range of meats on display cause the room to glow a provocative shade of pink, and the friendly smile on the face of the chubby, bald man behind the counter in his inexplicably pristine apron betrays a hidden political agenda.

"Welcome!" he yells, causing you to have to put conscious effort into not turning to see if he's addressing someone behind you. "What a lovely surprise to have a Protector visit my humble premises. Please, would you do me the honour of allowing me to show you the selection of carcasses I have out the back?"

Your expression must say it all, as he immediately berates himself.

"No, I suppose not. Stupid, Hobson, stupid. Well, please help yourself to a nice Bradfell pie, I'd be honoured to count you as a customer."

You take the pie, and leave onto Wall Street (turn to **65**).

165

You shuffle as if to aim for the gate to throw them off the scent, but then pick up the pace and hurl yourself forward through the streets until you are certain the boggarts are no longer following you.

Pausing to get your breath back, you gratefully take stock of your surroundings (turn to **65**).

166

"After you," he says, generously opening his arm to allow you to step through into the back room.

The moment your back foot crosses the threshold, a portcullis drops to the floor with a loud clang, and Olfric winces at the sound. He looks through the latticework with a pained expression.

"Look, I'm sorry," he says. "The simple fact is, you're worth more to me dead than alive, and I'm nothing if not pragmatic. You have some nice kit, and I never find myself in need of buyers. I'll give you some time to think, then you let me know how you want to go. You know, poison, starvation, beheading. I have something for everyone."

He closes the door, leaving you with your thoughts, as you steadily come to the conclusion that perhaps coming to Bradfell wasn't such a good idea, after all.

167

If you have the codeword *Cruncher*, turn immediately to 57.

If not, turn to 102.

168

The scribbles in the notepad look like they were formed underground by a particularly unintelligent dwarf who's lost the ability to see in the dark for a moment.

You can see that Hugnym had a moment of epiphany at one point, causing him to underline one of the items on his list. Or, at least, attempt to underline it. In his excitement, he seems to have just crossed the item out, making the list all but useless.

The image of the page should be used when searching the room to see if you can work out which item got him so excited. When you know the item, take the letters that make up its name and turn them each into a number using the code A=1, B=2, C=3, etc. Add them all together and turn to the section bearing this number. If you are right, the opening line will contain the name of the item.

Investigate the room	Turn to **363**
Leave onto Long Lane	Turn to **38**

169

As you walk away from the bandstand, you notice that the cobbles at your feet seem to have been arranged along this road more carefully than along others; the haphazard placing of stones to simply fill the space that characterises the rest of the city takes the form of a carefully-constructed pattern here.

Your attention clearly fixed to the ground, a young woman passing you helpfully suggests: "The shapes represent each of the three meadows you can see from the bandstand over there."

Nodding your thanks, you're left wondering whether the fact that you can count five different shapes has any meaning, as you arrive in Travellers Place (turn to **36**).

170

Grace Way continues along the length of the Fuming Fig, giving you glimpses in through the windows at local tavern frequenters of various shapes and sizes. Before too long, you've reached another road leading you up the hill (turn to **222**).

171

Clover Row in theory starts here, although within only a few paces you find yourself approaching what most locals would think of if you were to use that title, at the point where it meets another road (turn to 237).

172

As you wander around Petal Meadows, you take in the various verdant shades that stipple the surrounding trees and cast dancing shadows across the carefully choreographed flowerbeds.

A simple café has been set up in the centre of the park to serve the local residents and you find yourself gravitating towards it, and then hesitate when you see the proprietor, a greasy mound of sweat and monologue wearing a bushy moustache.

Will you approach the café's owner to ask if he has heard anything that might be of use to you (turn to 41), leave the park onto Faraway Road to the south (turn to 320) or onto Long Lane to the north-east (turn to 175)?

173

"Oh, well, never mind then. If you happen to come across anyone intelligent out there, send them in my direction, will you?"

He wanders off, leaving you to step back through the alleyway the way you came (turn to **347**).

174

This stretch of Wall Street benefits from sunlight at this time of day thanks to how straight it is, in comparison to other areas of the city.

A small crowd is huddled together in deep conversation up ahead, and you continue onward to reach them (turn to **80**).

175

You reach a large, impressive looking T-junction at which a brightly coloured street named Cobalt Lane leads away to the north-east under an arch that stretches from the buildings on one side to the other. The townsfolk pay no heed to the despicable teal cobblestones that line it, although in the distance you see them turn to an eye-watering gold, and have to look elsewhere to snap you out of the miniature trance you just felt sent into.

Not too far to the north-west down Long Lane you can see Main Gate, and a narrow alleyway directly opposite the end of Cobalt Lane offers a route into Petal Meadows, one of the green spaces in the town.

North-east: Cobalt Lane   Turn to **64**
South-east: Long Lane   Turn to **93**

South-west: into Petal Meadows   Turn to **172**
North-west: Long Lane   Turn to **339**

176

Privy is the traditional sport of Bradfell and the surrounding area, played typically by ladies more than men, with a high-profile competition each autumn.

Each round pits two Privy players, or Privates, against one another, who are positioned at opposite ends of a long room, seated on small, sturdy, wooden carts. They are armed with a short blade, blindfolded, and at the whistle wheel themselves towards their opponent, aiming to time their swing perfectly. The round concludes when blood is drawn.

"Ah, hello," an overweight woman greets you, whose ginger hair pokes out from under a small and unfashionable helmet. "I'm Margaret. Privy is hilarious, isn't it? Want a go?"

Agree to play Privy	Turn to **376**
Speak to the landlord	Turn to **218**
Join the drinkers	Turn to **397**
Leave north-east:	
Dragontoothache Passage	Turn to **234**
Leave south-east: Pride Pass	Turn to **222**

A round of pub games has always held a certain attraction for you, even with the riffraff of Bradfell, and you quickly tap into your experience and teach these locals a lesson.

As it turns out, their company is excellent. They seem to have survived so far in this city by having no grasp of reality whatsoever, and you find interacting with them a real joy. And the feeling is reciprocal; they ask you for another game, and when one of them offers to buy you a drink you think it would be rude to turn them down.

After a fun time with your newfound friends, you stand to leave. Whatever local brew they gave you seems to have gone to your head rather quicker than normal, but you still feel very much in control, and bid them good day before leaving into Travellers Place.

Record the codeword *Defarge*, and turn to **36**.

Clover Row is the name given to this set of steep steps that climb Bradfell Hill on its east side. An upper window in one of the narrow houses to your right opens, and you are fortunate to instinctively follow the flow of the crowd as they move away from the slop that suddenly falls to the floor, marking the front door and beginning its slow descent to the city wall below.

Physically feeling your disgust at the people that live here, you are grateful to have avoided that mess as you reach the top of the stairs (turn to **237**).

179

Memorial Lane plunges you into a surprising darkness after the bright colours of the crossroads behind you. Trying to avoid the puddles forming around you that seem to be getting deeper all the time, you plod on past several buildings until you arrive at the city wall (turn to **194**).

180

"Oh yeah, that's it!" the lady cries out in joy, counting out 459 Jimmies.

Jinfried mumbles something else you can't make out, and the entire group suddenly bursts into guffaws of laughter. Wiping tears from her eyes, the lady reaches into her bag.

"Here's your bottle. Thanks ever so much."

Taking hold of the bottle and stepping carefully away from the strange group, you think about what to do next.

Record the codeword *Carton*.

Speak to the landlord	Turn to **218**
Play a game of Privy	Turn to **176**
Leave north-east:	
Dragontoothache Passage	Turn to **234**

Leave south-east: Pride Pass Turn to **222**

181

Whoever came up with the name "Long Lane" didn't put much stock in originality. It stretches out ahead of you, eventually reaching the wall far off in the distance. It's one of the better roads in Bradfell, and before much walking you find yourself at a crossroads (turn to **38**).

182

Husband Graham's chamber is a grand affair, containing a decorative shrine, opulent drapes, paintings populating all the space on every wall, and three four-poster beds. A small, round table housing some rubbish and a small statue, inexplicably with no arms, looking somehow familiar yet alien, sits against one wall. Husband Graham is sitting staring at it as you enter.

"Oh, hello," he says, without much emotion. "You are welcome here. What can I do for you?"

You explain about Sir Julia's predicament, and he immediately brightens up.

"Oh yes, we can do something about that. It's quite special really. We've discovered that mashing medela herbs into this ointment and rubbing it all over the body does a fantastic job at addressing this issue. Would you like me to come and do it for you?"

You politely turn down his offer on Sir Julia's behalf, and take the ointment from him, hopeful that it will bring her back to full consciousness.

It doesn't take you long to retrace your steps across the city to find Sir Julia back in Sophia Park and, delicately, rub the ointment over every inch of her body that you can reach. Nothing you've not done before.

She stretches, shakes her head for a moment, and nods at you.

"Yes!" she declares. "That's done the trick! Wow, I need to get some of that back in Portsrood. Shall we have a drink to celebrate?"

Record the codeword *Theophile*.

Now, if you have the codeword *Gabelle*, turn to **315**.

If not, you consider where you will go next out of the park.

North-east: Faraway Road	Turn to **249**
North-west: Gait Gate	Turn to **344**
East: Clear Mist Lane	Turn to **234**
South: Wall Street	Turn to **130**

183

You are almost at the northernmost point of the city, standing ankle deep in a growing puddle of rainwater, which you can see flowing down Tortoise Walk from the south. Wall Street extends in both directions.

Anti-clockwise: Wall Street	Turn to **332**
Clockwise: Wall Street	Turn to **99**

South: Tortoise Walk   Turn to **328**

184

If you have the codeword *Alexandre*, turn immediately to **92**.

If not, turn to **256**.

185

You have reached a T-junction below the back of the City Hall, its banners gently licking the stones, creating eerie slapping noises that drift down to where you are standing.

The Saunter leads away from here to the south-west, immediately turning south, while Farewell Walk offers a short route to the north and Thunder Slop seems to drop dramatically away from you to the east. An old woman, halfway up, has paused to take in the abysmal view, refusing to let go of the ropes connected to the side of the buildings to aid walkers in their climb.

North: Farewell Walk	Turn to **212**
East: Thunder Slop	Turn to **285**
South-west: The Saunter	Turn to **3**

186

He looks confused. "You're serious? Well, your loss! Hey, see you around maybe."

He wanders away, slightly swaying as he goes, and you watch him until he has left the park. What will you do now?

Stroll around the park	Turn to **129**
Leave onto Freedom Lane	Turn to **167**
Leave into Brad Plaza	Turn to **242**

187

You pick up a likely looking pebble from the ground and toss it into the well. Your throw is a good one, and it falls without hitting the sides for a short time before returning an echoing plop, precisely as one would expect a well to.

Climb into the well	Turn to **225**
North-east: Shepherd Hill	Turn to **70**
South: Farewell Walk	Turn to **297**
North-west: Downwards Passage	Turn to **7**

188

The woman is waiting for you here, and you approach her with the necklace.

"Ah, you've got it. Lovely work. You've made an old lady very happy." She takes the necklace and hangs it round her neck, beaming with satisfaction.

"Now, I must find a way to thank you, mustn't I? Of course, I only have one possession now, so I'm going to use that to invest in the new bottle-selling business my friend at the Fuming Fig has set up. But for you, you'll find your reward with my other friend Malcolm. He lives among the pixies on Freedom Lane. Call out his name three times when you get there and he'll emerge. Like this: Malcolm! Malcolm! Malcolm! Tell him I sent you."

When you reach the place that the pixies live, if you'd like to call Malcolm's name three times, add 189 to the section number you are on, and turn to this new section.

She shuffles away, leaving you alone again (turn to 224).

(turn to 224)

189

This road is remarkably steep, demonstrated expertly as soon as you start to climb it by a man desperately trying to control a horse as it pulls a cart past you. That said, in this case the man's work seems to be to simply prevent the horse being run over by its own load.

As you follow the hill all the way to the top, the rain thankfully stops. You are shaking the droplets of water from your armour when you finally reach the corner of Brad Plaza (turn to 58).

(turn to 58)

190

You follow the gentle slope away from Long Lane, enjoying the view over the rolling hills that stretch away in front of you. It strikes you that if the buildings to your left weren't in the way, you might be able to see as far as the Sea of Sapphire, but as you turn to face in that direction you accidentally make eye contact with a scrawny old man leaning out of an upstairs window in the Sanctuary of Humility, wearing a vest that seems to be made of an old rag.

You hurriedly avert your eyes and move onward until you reach a T-junction (turn to **320**).

191

Entering Pride Pass conjures up an immediate sense of cognitive dissonance. The street is named after Stanothy Pride, an odd character in Bradfell's history, who made his name through attempting to make the city a place where – as far as you can tell – depravity was celebrated. The ugly murals depicting odd people doing odd things that cover the houses around you make you increasingly angry, and then you arrive at a T-junction that threatens to make you snap (turn to **327**).

192

He looks at you blankly for a moment.

"Well yes, of course I knew that. Why did she write it that way anyway? As if it was designed to confuse me. Anyway, thanks very much for helping, and now you can have this beautiful-" he cuts himself off, holding his hand in front of his face as he desperately tries to stop himself from laughing out loud, "I apologise. A beautiful, magic necklace. Hang it around your neck, and everyone will know you have good taste."

You find yourself thanking him and taking the necklace, leave him as he wanders off.

Record the codeword *Manette* and turn to **347**.

193
You have to admit that the fountain is a classic presentation of skilled stonework. You find it odd that Bradfell would put so much effort into decorating something so basic, when so much of their city is an embarrassment to be seen in, but you equally understand why the locals would appreciate meeting one another here.

Draw some water	Turn to **301**
Into the Travellers Rest	Turn to **198**
North-east: Velveteen Walk	Turn to **359**
West: Pride Pass	Turn to **399**
West: Thrice Meadow Lookout	Turn to **84**
To the Marked Gate	Turn to **201**
To Travellers Gate	Turn to **204**

194
The rain continues to fall as you reach one of the most popular places among pilgrims to Bradfell, The Blessed House of the Husband of Countless Wives and Sagas of Courageous Acts with Said Wives, known to locals as The Husband's House.

The Husband's House sits on the western side of Memorial Lane, which leads off to the south. The eastern side of the road boasts a large house covered in ivy, while Wall Street continues in both directions around the perimeter of the city.

Enter The Blessed House of the Husband of Countless Wives and Sagas of Courageous Acts with Said Wives   Turn to **115**

    Clockwise: Wall Street   Turn to **277**

    Anti-clockwise: Wall Street   Turn to **387**

    South: Memorial Lane   Turn to **139**

195

A hand swings out of nowhere and lands on your chest, stopping you unexpectedly in your tracks. Following it up the attached arm with your eyes, your vision lands on a man's unshaven face, criss-crossed with scars, his piercing eyes looking directly into yours with intrigue.

"Impressive," he says with a gravelly tone, using his other hand to trace the mark your bar fight earlier left on your face. "Yes, you look like the sort of person who'd like to know about the Legion Crushers. Oh, you've not heard of us? It's only the best fighters' guild in the country, and the most exclusive. I challenge you to join us for a bout."

Of course, to turn down the gauntlet dropped at your feet would be a matter of chivalry and honour. He walks through an unassuming door in the wall, and you follow him in and down a flight of stairs, where you find a fighting ring has been drawn up in chalk on the floor. Twenty or so characters are gathered around the perimeter in small groups, and a low growl emerges as you reach the bottom.

"Welcome our latest contender!" your new friend announces, and the crowd gives a light cheer. "Pick your opponent."

Two of the characters have stepped into the ring, both looking at you with a combination of fear and cockiness. One is an overweight man with a drooping moustache, while the other is a skinny runt of a boy. Neither looks like being a particular challenge for you, although you've been in enough encounters to know that it would be a mistake to consider either an easy opponent.

Will you choose the large man (turn to **206**) or the small boy (turn to **342**)?

196

It's not following the rules dictated by Duke Morrison de Livery, but it's certainly effective. His pained expression communicating a mental battle in which he tries to convince himself to keep on fighting in the face of an overwhelmingly good reason not to, you are pleased when his face descends to the floor and a satisfied cheer from the crowd confirms that you have won.

"Good work," the man from outside says, clapping as he closes the distance to you. "I knew you'd fit right in. Oh, hold still a moment." He holds his hand towards you, palm facing outwards, and mutters something: "*Rastiad endoe sayeltiad ponaytos.* That'll do it. You now carry a magic mark so all will know you've been victorious here. Well, all who matter, anyway."

Satisfied that you've done what you needed to, you return up the stairs and walk outside.

Record the codeword *Alexandre* and turn to **21**.

197

You are almost at the furthest point west within the city walls, at the foot of Clear Mist Lane, which ascends the Bradfell hill to the north-east.

Clockwise: Wall Street	Turn to **245**
Anti-clockwise: Wall Street	Turn to **362**
North-east: Clear Mist Lane	Turn to **209**

198 ❑

If the box above is ticked, turn immediately to turn to **220**.

If not, put a tick in it now and turn to **251**.

199

As the road moves away from Brad Plaza, the faces in the crowd begin to change away from those involved in the entertainment and political spheres, and towards those who keep the town ticking. The uniforms here are much more functional, and you get a sense that this is true Bradfell.

The smells of cooking food waft along the street, and the sounds of practical conversations fill your ears as you reach a T-junction (turn to 213).

200

You splash water into the slumbering face of Sir Julia right as she is halfway through a particularly loud snore, interrupting the noise and causing her to inhale the liquid.

Coughing and spluttering into her beard, spots of water and whatever she was drinking last night being projected in every direction, she flails around for a moment before seeing you and calming herself down. Taking in your surroundings for a moment, she looks backs at you with a pleased expression.

"Well," she says, a rasping sound betraying her need to drink some of the water that is now dripping from her face, "I've woken up in worse places! Ooh," she suddenly interrupts herself, "I don't feel very well."

She lies back down, groaning and unable to say any more, and you wonder where you might find some medicine. Perhaps from a temple? You have to admit, the idea of making her suffer a bit longer gives you a satisfying feeling of justice.

Record the codeword *Foulon* and turn to 22.

The Marked Gate bears its name thanks to the odd glyphs that have marked its mantle. Philosophers, priests and academics have studied them to within an inch of their life to no avail, not helped by the fact that an ancient limerick that originally sat inscribed on it can still be seen through the supernatural addition. Most debate about the markings now revolves around which elements belong to the original *There Was a Dull Oaf Named Mark*, which had given the gate its original name of the Mark Gate. Confusion prevails everywhere apart from within Bradfell itself.

The Marked Gate sits pride of place at the southernmost tip of the triangular Travellers Place, which has in its centre a peculiarly decorative well. The Meadow Parade stretches directly north from here to Velveteen Walk, passing Thrice Meadow Lookout on the way. Travellers Gate is in the other corner of Travellers Place, while the Travellers Rest inn is the grand building on the north-east edge of the Place.

A Gates Carriage sits by you, ready to take you to one of the other gates around the city perimeter.

Investigate the well	Turn to **193**
Into the Travellers Rest	Turn to **198**
North: end of Velveteen Walk	Turn to **36**
North: end of Thrice Meadow	

Lookout	Turn to **201**
To Travellers Gate	Turn to **204**
Clockwise: Wall Street	Turn to **32**
Onto the Gates Carriage	Turn to **10**

202

You lie down on the bed, which is extremely uncomfortable. As you lie there, you wonder whether this handful of adjacent planks covered in a scratchy cloth would actually be defined as a bed, but you stop your thoughts before they confuse you.

No-one comes, and you feel like you ought to do something. Will you try to escape through the window (turn to **233**), shout to get someone's attention (turn to **230**), or wait a bit more (turn to **284**)?

203

"I end up with all sorts here," Olfric says, a wry smile playing across his face. "What sort of thing are you after?"

What will you say you are looking for?

A necklace	Turn to **63**
A set of lockpicks	Turn to **349**
A weapon	Turn to **91**

204

Travellers Gate stands proudly as the only exit that leads directly to Portsrood, although its heavily barred state and grumpy-looking guards communicate strongly that no-one will be leaving by it quite yet.

Travellers Place extends from the gate outwards to the west, while a winding road bearing the sign Politicians Regret steadily climbs the hill from here to the north.

North: Politicians Regret	Turn to **152**
West: Travellers Place	Turn to **36**
Anti-clockwise: Wall Street	Turn to **388**
Onto the Gates Carriage	Turn to **10**

205

The hill you climb is not particularly forgiving, and your calves begin to ache with the relentless walking you've been doing. Maybe you deserve a nice massage when you return to Portsrood.

The idea of a future in which you're not in Bradfell vivid in your mind, you continue until you reach another junction (turn to **222**).

206

You step into the ring, and your opponent grins through his moustache, his jowls wobbling as he does so.

"Go ahead then!" the man from outside calls, and before you have a chance to set yourself, the beast has started running at you. With his weight behind him, momentum will be on his side.

Will you brace yourself for impact (turn to 143), lightly jab your fist into his oncoming face to stop him in his tracks (turn to 232), or plant an uppercut on his chin (turn to 324)?

207

You are just thinking how awfully dirty the road is beneath your feet, when a spot of rain appears on one of the cobbles ahead of you. A second follows it, and rapidly you find yourself in a torrential storm, the dirt on the floor quickly turning to mud that starts to creep up your usually spotless and shiny greaves.

A level of grumpiness setting in, you hurry to the gate ahead of you (turn to 108).

208

Whatever resolution this hill is named after, it was not to make traversing the city any simpler. The cobbles jutting out at strange angles as if intricately choreographed around ancient ley lines, you find yourself having to concentrate surprisingly hard as you ascend.

A sense of accomplishment accompanying your climb, you reach a junction halfway up the hill (turn to 184).

As you begin to climb the hill you notice, much to your surprise, that the houses on either side of you seem to be reasonably clean. It strikes you that the entrance to Sophia Park on your left probably has something to do with it – living this close to probably the nicest green space in the city must require a relatively high amount of wealth.

Pleased that you are surrounded by your sort of people, will you head into Sophia Park (turn to **34**), or continue up the hill to a crossroads (turn to **234**)?

The well looks as harmless and dull as anything else in this city. Its mouth is easily large enough to allow a person entry, and so you consider climbing down to see what secrets its base might hold.

Climb into the well	Turn to **225**
Drop a pebble into the well	Turn to **187**
North-east: Shepherd Hill	Turn to **70**
South: Farewell Walk	Turn to **297**
North-west: Downwards Passage	Turn to **7**

Her fist passes over your head, the momentum behind it carrying her so far forward that she ends up spinning herself away from you.

Will you kick her in the back now you have the advantage (turn to **373**), or wait for her to turn around to get a hit into her face (turn to **312**)?

212

If you have the codeword *Sydney,* turn immediately to **351**.

If not, turn to **271**.

213 ❑

If the box above is ticked, turn immediately to **158**.

If not, put a tick in it now, and turn to **311**.

214

When you mention the cleaver, his expression changes from a welcoming smile to one of concerned anger.

"Yes," he bellows, "That cleaver's mine. I'd been wondering where it had gone. I told Keegan about it yesterday. And do you know, normally I'd have you talk to my assistant Manfred because he cleans and packs them up at the end of the day, but he doesn't work on Knoffdays. He tends to spend his days off at the Fuming Fig I think, you know, on the other side of Sophia Park."

It looks like Manfred holds the information you'll need to get to the bottom of this. Thanking the butcher for his time, you head out onto Wall Street (turn to **65**).

215

"Oh," Sir Julia suddenly pipes up, carefully considering her next words. "Yes, it does look a bit familiar in here. Yes, Manfred was talking about making some money or some such nonsense. It all sounded a bit fishy now I remember. We even went back to his place for a bit. Hey! Wouldn't it be a good idea to find it? If only I could remember where it was. Do you know, I'm sure I'll know it when I see it. It was right by a city gate that had a great big sculpture above it in the shape of two entwined people. Shall we head out?" She starts marching towards the exit, perhaps wanting to avoid you discovering any more of her antics from the previous night.

When you reach the location at which you think Manfred's house sits, add 50 to the section number and turn to this new section.

Join a group of drinkers	Turn to **397**
Play a round of Privy	Turn to **176**
Leave north-east:	
Dragontoothache Passage	Turn to **234**
Leave south-east: Pride Pass	Turn to **222**

"Oh, that's easy," he begins. "I was born and brought up in Backwale, a small village to the north of here, famed for its puddings. My childhood was free of worries until my twelfth Birthday, when everything changed.

"I lost my parents in a robbery gone wrong, and I was left alone and forgotten. I had to learn how to survive on my own, but I knew one thing: I wasn't going to follow my parents into a life of crime.

"I dedicated my life to enforcing the law, firstly as part of the Backwale militia and then I felt the call to the big city. And that's why I'm here today!"

Realising he's finished, you thank him and hurry out of his office, not wanting to endure any more pointless storytelling.

Ask to report a crime	Turn to **396**
Ask for information or equipment	Turn to **378**
Leave the building	Turn to **259**

You crouch without warning just as he's about to headbutt you and his movement carries him forwards and over your back. You stand instinctively, victoriously observing your downed opponent, and the crowd around you cheers in delight at the spectacle.

"Good work," the man from outside says, clapping as he closes the distance to you. "I knew you'd fit right in. Oh, hold still a moment." He holds his hand towards you, palm facing outwards, and mutters something: *"Rastiad endoe sayeltiad ponaytos.* That'll do it. You now carry a magic mark so all will know you've been victorious here. Well, all who matter, anyway."

Satisfied that you've done what you needed to, you return up the stairs and walk outside.

Record the codeword *Alexandre* and turn to **21**.

218

If you want to ask about a particular person, turn the letters in their name into numbers using the code A=1, B=2, C=3, etc, add them all up and turn to that section number. If not, the landlord doesn't leave his stool, but is quite happy to have a conversation.

"I heard a rumour recently, now you come to mention it," he says. "A group in here the other day was talking about a secret club that meets behind the City Hall. They were saying that entry's only granted to those who bear the scars of a brawl, but they were all Portsrood pansies – begging your pardon, I'm sure – and none of them had been in a street fight. Oh, excuse me."

He follows the call of duty to help his staff change an ale barrel, leaving you alone at the bar.

Join the drinkers   Turn to **397**

Play a round of Privy	Turn to **176**
Leave north-east:	
Dragontoothache Passage	Turn to **234**
Leave south-east: Pride Pass	Turn to **222**

219

As you reach the T-junction, an old woman with a long beard emerges from the crowd and crows at you: "Oh, the bravest of knights! Could you help an old woman please?"

Your chivalrous nature prevents you from ignoring her, and you express your willingness to serve this hideous old crone, a shiver of pride breezing through you.

"Oh, thank you most kindly," she chatters away at you. "You see, I dropped my handkerchief just here a moment ago, and now I can't find it."

You immediately see the grubby handkerchief a few paces away in the mouth of an alley, and step forward to retrieve it. As you do so, you suddenly find yourself surrounded by a crowd of street urchins, who start bundling you, pushing you from behind, deeper into the alleyway!

You struggle, but there are too many of them, and within a minute or two you are driven down some steps and in the basement of a dark, dank house.

"Ah, ah, ah, welcome," a skinny old man says in greeting, his long, ginger beard dancing with every syllable. "Mmm, mmm, mmm, it's always helpful to have a live subject to practice on, and what a fine specimen you are."

Before you can protest, and despite you struggling every step of the way, you are taken further into the building and locked in a small cell. The footsteps of your captors fade into the distance, and you take in your surroundings.

The small room contains a bed, a small table and chair, and a high window that throws the only light available towards you. The window is barred, and the whole place smells like damp; you imagine that when it rains the water flows directly in through the window.

Will you see if you can escape by trying to pull the bars out of the window (turn to **233**), lie down on the bed and wait until your captors come back (turn to **202**), or start to shout to get someone's attention (turn to **230**)?

220

You are in the Travellers Rest, where you spent last night. Una Wright is busying herself around you, wiping tables, serving patrons, even this early in the day, and occasionally shouting orders to the workers from the brewery and bakery that sit on either side of the inn. You conclude they must produce the food and drink you remember tucking into yesterday, although you quickly try to push those memories away from your mind as nausea begins to kick in.

A group of old men and young women is playing some games around a circular table to one side, and it looks like they've left a space for newcomers to join them.

Will you join in their game (turn to 177), or head outside into Travellers Place (turn to 36)?

221

The Duke of Vanhelm is actually quite nicely decked out inside, with a large U-shaped bar surrounded by various tables and tiny snugs.

"Oh!" a voice calls out as you enter, and a lady in a tidy uniform hurries over to you. "I'm so sorry to keep you waiting. How exciting to have one of the Protectors with us. Please, a drink on the house, or perhaps a meal?"

You have to admit, you are quite hungry. Will you agree to have a meal (turn to 82), or make your excuses and leave (turn to 357)?

222

The T-junction you find yourself at is located halfway up Bradfell hill, although you can't get any higher from here.

The Steep gives you an option down towards the city wall to the south-west, while Pride Pass and Grace Way offer routes around the hill to the east and north-west respectively. On the corner of The Steep and Grace Way, the Fuming Fig, with its thatched roof and dancing patrons outside, is a large inn that beckons you in with its sense of life, and scent of stale beer and pipe smoke.

Into the Fuming Fig Turn to **336**

East: Pride Pass	Turn to **191**
South-west: The Steep	Turn to **228**
North-west: Grace Way	Turn to **156**

223

You have walked for only a few paces before noticing that this road feels exceptionally straight, and exceptionally long. To be fair, everything in Bradfell feels longer to you than it ought to be, so perhaps that's your prejudice talking, but probably not.

The houses along this road are uniform and predictable, which would feel professional and appropriate if they were pleasant to look at, but they're not. Looking to your left, you realise that from the top floor they must command a good view out of Bradfell to the west, almost as far as the Thermogrand Hills. You conclude that this is probably one of the better places to live, as at least you don't have to be staring at the interior of the city the whole time.

After far longer than you'd like, you arrive at the opposite end of Laughing Walk (turn to **320**).

224

You are standing at the westernmost corner of the shocking white Sanctuary of Humility, at a point where the long Faraway Road meets Laughing Walk, which leads along the western wall of the Sanctuary to the south.

North: Petal Meadows Turn to **172**
North-east: Faraway Road Turn to **393**
South: Laughing Walk Turn to **49**
South-west: Faraway Road Turn to **365**
Into the Sanctuary of Humility Turn to **26**

225

You test the rope a couple of times by putting your full weight on it against the side of the well, and it provides a good sense of strength and sturdiness. You extend it to its full length and carefully grab hold of it, transferring your body one part at a time, until you are comfortable you are on.

Your descent is steady, and the damp radiating from the moss-covered walls around you gives your skin a cool clamminess that, while not entirely pleasant, is certainly no worse than the general feeling of Bradfell above ground.

It isn't long before you reach the end of the rope. You can see the faint sunlight delicately glinting off the surface of the water below you, but the rope won't extend any further. If you like, you can let go of the rope and drop into the water (turn to **42**).

If not, there is nothing else for you to do other than climb up and leave the junction.

North-east: Shepherd Hill Turn to **70**
South: Farewell Walk Turn to **297**
North-west: Downwards Passage Turn to **7**

226

You have reached Lowly Gate, situated at an odd point in the city wall where it juts out from the bottom of Slumgate as if to launch into a major road, before immediately ending at the heavy portcullis.

The crowd here is a throng, as locals try to get from one part of the city to another using either the Gates Carriage or perhaps simply the ease of walking down the hill to reach this point.

The Lowly Gate itself is decorated with carvings of Bradfell's history, telling in particular the story of the Bradfell poor being housed in the north-east of the city and then protected from the elite within Bradfell proper by the city wall. The gate arch is topped with a delightful sculpture of a pair of conjoined twins, in memory of the curse of Madam Anndrasdan, whose name has been forbidden to be spoken within the city.

Within a few moments of you arriving, a Gates Carriage pulls up and shouts for passers-by to board.

Clockwise: Wall Street	Turn to **395**
Anti-clockwise: Wall Street	Turn to **207**
West: Slumgate	Turn to **40**
Onto the Gates Carriage	Turn to **10**

227

A huge smile suddenly breaks out on his face.

"Eestrakkaltir!" he yells, throwing his arms around you in ecstasy. "Now, you must come with me. It's urgent."

He starts to walk away, clearly expecting you – or, at least, this Eestrakkaltir, whoever that is – to follow him. You've been mistaken for someone else, but this has worked out well for you in the past. Will you follow him (turn to **367**), or use the chance to duck outside (turn to **357**)?

228

As you proceed down the hill, you see a local heading in your direction. You try to cross to the other side, but he does the same thing and you find yourself cornered. Tugging at the peak of his woollen cap, he greets you with an accent you're sure the uneducated rabble would describe as "quaint".

"Hello there!" he says, cheerily. "Enjoying your stay in Bradfell? O' course you are. Who wouldn't? Well, I suppose the pixie haters aren't too keen, but there's no pleasing them now, is there? With the right charm, they're no problem, are they?"

Noncommittally agreeing in principle, you push past him and don't stop moving until you reach another junction (turn to **267**).

229

You recognise these grounds from the previous evening, although you have to admit it's a bit more impressive in the daylight. The birds circle around your head, flitting from tree to tree and singing snippets of songs to one another with the freedom that only birds have.

A brief walk around the grounds reveals that the trees here are purely here for their looks, surrounding the manor you ate in yesterday evening, although the grey clouds overhead make you wonder whether you may need to use them for shelter in a moment.

There is nothing else here of interest and so you leave onto Slumgate.

West, up Slumgate   Turn to **58**
East, down Slumgate   Turn to **226**

230

You start to scream at the top of your lungs, and straight away hear the bang of a door opening outside, and footsteps approaching the door.

"Hey!" a voice from directly outside the door. "Keep that noise down. I'm not joking, if you do that again, I'll cast a spell on you."

A spell? you think to yourself. *Surely that's an empty threat?* You're not sure whether to risk it. Will you now try to escape through the window (turn to **233**), lie down on the bed and just wait for someone to come for you (turn to **284**), or will you shout again (turn to **299**)?

Afterlife Alley does not paint a positive picture of what awaits the eternal soul of a Bradfell resident.

The soot-covered walls offer a striking high contrast to the stone walls that hem you in on either side, making the poverty somehow picturesque, and you wonder if you could bring some artificial elements of this back to Portsrood with you.

After walking for a while, you arrive at a junction (turn to **65**).

The light crunch of his nose squashing you're your is pleasing to your ears without being pleasant. His stomping feet continue to try running into the air while his head remains attached to your knuckles, causing him to levitate for a moment before crashing to the floor.

"Good work," the man from outside says, clapping as he closes the distance to you. "I knew you'd fit right in. Oh, hold still a moment." He holds his hand towards you, palm facing outwards, and mutters something: *"Rastiad endoe sayeltiad ponaytos.* That'll do it. You now carry a magic mark so all will know you've been victorious here. Well, all who matter, anyway."

Satisfied that you've done what you needed to, you return up the stairs and walk outside.

Record the codeword *Alexandre* and turn to **21**.

233

You take a couple of deep breaths, preparing yourself for the test of strength that awaits you, and grab hold of two of the bars.

Almost disappointingly, the rust that you originally had perceived to be delicately coating the outside of the bars turns out to have eaten deep inside them, and it's all you can do to avoid being covered by the dust as they easily snap and crumble in your hands.

The bars out of the way, you easily climb up and crawl away from the building, through some shrubbery to emerge into a large grassy area surrounded by trees (turn to **172**).

234 ☐

If you have the codeword *Pross* and the box above is not ticked, put a tick in it now and turn to **160**.

If you do not have the codeword *Pross,* or the box above is already ticked, turn to **4**.

235

"I'll leave you to it then," he says, waddling back behind a desk and starting to write on a piece of paper.

You look around the shop, at the array of broken clocks, second-hand books, broken furniture and soiled clothes. None of this is any use to you, and you don't have any money to spend on it in any case.

Bidding Olfric a good day, to which he doesn't respond, you leave (turn to **95**).

236

The Phoenix and Pheasant is everything that Sir Julia is attracted to: a tavern. In fact, it's as if the very essence of the idea of a tavern has materialised into reality; this tavern is more tavern-like than any other tavern you can think of.

You pause your thinking for a moment, as the word "tavern" strikes you as being particularly peculiar, when the publican, an overweight woman with a half-cleaned tankard in her hand, leans towards you.

"Alright?" she demands.

The way in which you maintain your composure even as she startles you gives you a sense of achievement, and you respond chivalrously before asking if she's seen your fellow Protector.

"Can't you see I'm too busy to deal with your trifles?" she responds, a biting anger cutting through her words. You have to admit to yourself that you can't see any sense of busyness about her at all. "If this Sir Julia has been here – I think you'll find it's pronounced *Hulia* now you're up in Bradfell – one of these two will have seen her. They never leave this place."

She indicates two of the dozen or so grumpy people in the room, who turn their tiny eyes towards you as you approach. They introduce themselves as Gwendolyn Glover, a stocky woman in her mid-forties trying to stab the table in front of her with a dagger, and Oswald Baker, a plump man reading a newspaper who clearly never picked up that leather is now out of fashion.

Which will you ask about Sir Julia? Gwendolyn Glover (turn to **46**), or Oswald Baker (turn to **43**)?

237

If you have both codewords *Evremonde* and *Bernard*, turn immediately to **384**. If you have neither or only one of those codewords, turn to **116**.

238

Husband Graham looks pleased to see you as you approach him.

"Ah, welcome to my home!" he gushes, his neatly trimmed beard perfectly framing his handsome features. "I assume my wives have been making you comfortable? But not too comfortable, I hope! You know, the thing about wives..."

He launches into an entirely inappropriate monologue purely intended, it would appear, to make you feel extremely awkward. If that is its goal, it hits the mark perfectly. He drones on about the importance of fidelity, a woman's rightful place, how jealousy is an attractive feature, and his previous night's activities, none of which you needed to hear.

The moment he pauses for breath, you make your excuses and leave in a hurry. Will you duck out through the back into Black Dragon Grounds (turn to 47), or head onto Wall Street (turn to 194)?

239

You struggle to stop yourself feeling utterly miserable as you trudge along in the rain, your sound of your clanking armour and the splashes of puddles reverberating off the walls that close in on either side of you.

The road looks like it bends round to the south-east a few houses ahead, but not before you reach a T-junction (turn to 194).

240

You are not known as a hero for nothing, and jumping while being tied to a chair is something that seems to come naturally to you. You close the distance to the upturned sledge quite quickly, and then disaster strikes.

Jumping while tied to a chair on a flat surface is all well and good, but this floor is not flat. As your chair leg lands in a small hole, the chair tips over on its side, taking you with it. You are unable to lift your hands out of the ropes to stop your neck landing neatly on the exposed blade, decapitating you instantly.

241

You arch your back and put your full force behind a slap that is severely cushioned by Sir Julia's vast beard.

Shrugging your shoulders as you remember that this approach has never worked in the past either, you head out to find some water (turn to 22).

242

You are standing in the centre of Brad Plaza. The grand steps leading up into the City Hall on the east side still bear the evidence of last night's festivities, while the theatre directly opposite is adorned with coloured banners, enticing local residents to spend their saved-up coins on manufactured entertainment that would be an embarrassment in even the cheapest theatres in Portsrood.

Crowds of people bustle around you in every direction, their feet tracing the well-trodden routes across the square, particularly between two grand arches that stand on either side of the theatre. The title "Preachers Corner" is emblazoned across the archway at the opening to Long Lane in the north-west corner, while its sister in the south-west corner proudly carries the name "Travellers Court", leading down towards the Travellers Rest, where you stayed last night.

Similar arches also stand on either side of the City Hall, "Slum Corner" to its left and "Politicians Court" to its right.

Into the City Hall	Turn to **358**
North-east: Slum Corner	Turn to **58**
South-east: Politicians Court	Turn to **2**
South-west: Travellers Court	Turn to **29**
North-west: Preachers Corner	Turn to **161**

243

You extend your arms in front of you suddenly, but the wiry body of the boy squirms in between them, if anything closing the small remaining distance between you.

He smiles, his array of gleaming white teeth betraying either a privileged upbringing or having taken them from a wealthy victim. "You must think I'm an idiot to fall for that," he whispers, and then you feel the sharp corner of his fist connect with your stomach.

At least, it begins with a sharp corner of a fist, but it is then that you feel the extension of a hidden blade worming its way through your armour and entering your internal organs.

The echoing sounds of bloodthirsty cheers crown your dying moments.

244

Leaving the troll statue and the confusing crowd behind you, you make your way north, following the city wall, carefully stepping around the puddles that formed during the downpour earlier in the day.

Passers-by nod at you in respect, and you dutifully ignore them all; naturally, they are not worthy of your time.

After several boringly nondescript buildings, you reach another T-junction (turn to **357**).

245

You continue along Wall Street, and then continue some more, as it takes you out to the left and then back to the right.

You notice a city gate up ahead just as a cry from behind you of "Look out!" gives you the split second's notice you need to avoid being run over by the Gates Carriage. You're sure it's never gone that quickly when you're on it.

After a short time more, you reach the gate (turn to **344**).

246

Politicians Regret is a bright collection of expensive-looking houses along a zigzag that descends the hill. Around each of the corners smug, relaxed people slowly saunter, commenting to one another on theories surrounding the closure of the gates.

A short walk later and you arrive at the base of the hill, where the street meets a city gate (turn to 204).

247

"I'm afraid he's not here," one of the wives explains to you. "He went to a meeting in Sumtumner Manor, something to do with signing a trade agreement with Portsrood. You know, it's the big house in the middle of Sumtumner Grounds."

To enter the house, add 150 to the section number you end up in when you reach Sumtumner Grounds.

Now, will you leave through the back into Black Dragon Grounds (turn to 47) or through the front onto Wall Street (turn to 194)?

248

"Very well," he says, "Your loss, I suppose."

He keeps his eye on you as he lifts his glass to his mouth again (turn to 5).

249

You have reached a T-junction on Faraway Road, which reaches up the hill to the north-east and down to the west. Fabled Alley offers an option to the south-east, where the houses look particularly proud to overlook the grand Sophia Park, situated directly south of your current location.

North-east: Faraway Road	Turn to **56**
South: Fabled Alley	Turn to **16**
South-west: into Sophia Park	Turn to **34**
West: Faraway Road	Turn to **383**

250

Storming through the door, you clatter right into the shady character, who turns out to be a short-haired, dark girl, begging for her life.

"I'm so sorry," she squeals, tears edging their way into her eyes. "I didn't mean to, they told me to get you to chase me down here."

You are about to ask who, when a thump on your head prematurely ends your conversation (turn to **11**).

251

The door swings open easily, and you step into the bar of the Travellers Rest. As you step past the chair in which you were sitting yesterday evening, faint memories of your night float across your mind, and you rapidly experience a

recollection of the highs of hilarity and a shameful, despairing embarrassment.

Casting those away from you, you move to the carpeted stairs – quite a luxury in Bradfell – and take them two at a time, your armour clattering around you, and knock on the door to Sir Julia's room.

It opens at your touch, revealing an untidy mess as you'd expect, bedclothes strewn across the window frame and the bedpan balanced precariously on a portrait of Bradfell's most famous mayor, but no Sir Julia. You ponder for a moment and then head back downstairs.

The publican, Una, is wiping down a table as you descend, and you ask if she's seen Sir Julia this morning.

"Not today," comes her reply. "I don't think she came back after, well, you know, after last night. She was spending a lot of time with that young lad Tom."

Your memory suddenly kicks into gear again. Yes, Sir Julia has a tendency to find unassuming young men and take advantage of them.

"They probably went back to Tom's place. His parents run the Phoenix and Pheasant, in the temple district."

It looks like grabbing Sir Julia is going to be slightly less straightforward than you first assumed.

Record the codeword *Darnay* and turn to **220**.

252

The constant flow of young fathers milling around you aimlessly, constantly stopping and rubbing their eyes as if no-one has ever had it as bad as them, is beginning to get you down. You find yourself leaning against a decorative signpost pointing up the hill with the simple description "The Steep". You prepare to move on.

North-east: The Steep	Turn to **281**
Clockwise: Wall Street	Turn to **272**
Anti-clockwise: Wall Street	Turn to **319**

253

A lady dressed in a pristine dress greets you as you enter, explaining that you will need to exchange some cash for chips if you would like to enter.

Boldly, you smile and withdraw the chip from your pocket, offering it to her as your ticket for entry.

"Yes, that's the sort of thing," she says cheerily. "You'll just need another nine of those to place the minimum bet, as it's only worth one half gold piece. Do you have any more?" You explain that you don't, but she takes it from you anyway, the smile on her face remaining in place as if painted on. "Never mind," she continues, "do you have some cash to buy some more, or – wait a minute!"

The smile turning immediately into a look of shock, she turns and runs through the dark curtain behind her, returning a few moments later accompanied by a broad man with a handlebar moustache and a monocle.

"Wow!" the man says, his gruff voice making it sound like this level of excitement is quite foreign to him. "I must thank you for bringing this back. This is no normal chip. This is the first we ever made here, and it was stolen some time ago. Come with me."

He leads you through the curtain and into a dark room, dimly lit by candles across a small selection of almost empty tables. A glass-fronted cabinet on one wall glows from the magical stones laid into its corners, glittering from a couple of small trophies and statuettes. He pulls a tiny key from his pocket and unlocks the door, carefully placing the wooden chip in a gap clearly intended for it.

"Home again!" he says, then turns to you and throws his arms around you in a bear hug you do not reciprocate. "I'll have a word with the staff. You're welcome here any time. Bring cash!"

He escorts you out and bids you farewell before returning back through the curtain, leaving you outside to decide where to go next.

North-east: The Steep	Turn to **205**
South-east: Thrice Meadow	
Lookout	Turn to **85**
South-west: The Steep	Turn to **278**

254

"Oh," he says, caught off guard. "I'm ever so sorry. Please, allow me to buy you another drink."

He shuffles off, a look of slight confusion on your face, and a minute later another ale has found its way onto the table in front of you.

You finish up, confused about the encounter but grateful for the sustenance, and make your way outside again (turn to **357**).

255

It's as if this terrible version of Portsrood Palace had been designed to make it easy to break into. The passage into the park is dark, and a hole next to the building is large enough for you to walk straight through without being seen. A couple of minutes later, and you're inside.

You navigate through the rooms, accidentally breaking a vase on your way although the state of the whole thing makes you think no-one would notice – in fact, it brings a nice bit of variety to the place now you think about it.

You find the master bedroom as instructed, and the drawer in the dresser opens without the need for a key.

And then you realise that you don't have the forged deed – hiding this one would defeat the purpose of you being here, and put the future of the building in the hands of the foolish Council of Bradfell!

You cautiously make your way out again successfully, determined to return once you've connected with the Green Teabag (turn to **340**).

256

You are at the midpoint of Thrice Meadow Lookout, and you ascend the bandstand erected here to get a glimpse over the green fields that lead south towards the coast. Far off to the east, the towers of Portsrood Castle are just visible on the horizon, teasing you.

North: Lilting Lane   Turn to **269**

East: Thrice Meadow Lookout   Turn to **169**

South: Resolution Hill   Turn to **15**

West: Thrice Meadow Lookout   Turn to **323**

257

The slight passage that leads out of the park provides an area covered with vines, intended to provide shade in the sun and protection from the elements in the rain and snow.

As it is, the plants and damp and have turned the floor into a slippery, mushy path of leaves, insects and mushrooms. Careful not to fall, you make your way through and out onto Long Lane (turn to **340**).

258

You call out Malcolm's name at the top of your lungs three times, and a tall, slender man files out of a house at your side.

"Alright, alright, there's no need to shout. Was it that woman again, sending people in my direction for helping her out?"

Something in your expression must give away that you are indeed one of those people, and Malcolm sighs.

"No problem, I suppose she said I'd reward you, didn't she? Well, here you go." He moves back inside his house, looks around, and then picks something up before turning back to you. "This is a gambling chip. It's worth money, but only within Lord Tunpet's Gambling Den on The Steep. Take it there and you can exchange it for cash. You're welcome."

He walks back inside his house, muttering to himself and leaving you to turn over the carefully carved piece of wood you now hold in your hands.

Record the codeword *Jourdan* and turn back to **69**.

259

If you have the codeword *Jacques*, and do not have the codeword *Barsad*, turn immediately to **353**.

If you do not have the codeword *Jacques*, or if you do have the codeword *Barsad*, turn to **145**.

260

After a short walk, she enters a well-kept little house and you follow her in. Through a narrow but well-lit passage she leads you into a dining room. Large windows reveal a view of three large meadows stretching away in different directions, and the pretty woman, backlit by the sunlight streaming in, turns to look at you.

"Pardon me," she says, and then closes her eyes. You wonder what she is doing, when you notice her hands beginning to vibrate, then her arms – within seconds, her entire body is shaking and you step forward to assist when the shaking stops.

"Oh, that's better," she says, although the pretty young lady is no longer pretty or young. In fact, she is perhaps the foulest creature you've ever seen. Her now lopsided features boast unfortunate warts and prominent veins, an unattractive shock of grey hair, and a wizened old body that repulses you. Looking at your expression, she bursts into laughter.

"Ha ha ha ha!" she screeches, the hag's voice now fully transformed. "I do love so much that reaction. That's the face my late husband pulled too. Enough about him though. Listen. You can give me a hand now you're here. I have a new destiny for you, and you'll find it easily enough. There's a room in a house that you're going to go to, and the room contains many riches, but you'd never know it to look at it. The riches are hidden in a secret safe built into the wall. You'll find it if you look. The safe has a code, remember this. The code is 42375. Find your way in, and your destiny will reveal itself to you. Now, out you go."

Still stunned into stupidity by what's just happened, you find yourself being led out and pushed into the road by the crone, who slams the door behind you (turn to **256**).

261

"Oh, have they?" he says, looking as if you'd just told him you were planning on eating your firstborn for dinner. "Perhaps that's why, then."

He walks off, leaving you confused. You finish up, and make your way out when you're ready (turn to **357**).

You walk through the door and are greeted by a lady in what would even be described as a smart dress in Portsrood. You nod to yourself in approval and move to step past her, but she holds her hand up.

"Oh, you'll need to exchange some cash for chips, I'm afraid," she says. You do your best to convince her that you have no need for cash and that she should allow you entry anyway due to your birth line, but she is having none of it and you are forced to admit defeat, leaving the building.

Frustrated, and wondering where one gets their hands on this cash, you decide where to go next.

North-east: The Steep	Turn to **205**
South-east: Thrice Meadow Lookout	Turn to **85**
South-west: The Steep	Turn to **278**

263

You leave the crowds behind and step out into the eerily quiet road, following it around the bend. You do your best to stop the nausea caused by the rain pouring down various unappetising shades of brown, while the sound of a distant bell reminds you that elsewhere in the city life is continuing.

As you continue, the clouds part, and you are still dripping wet as you reach another junction (turn to **167**).

264

The rain continues to fall as you step onto the yellow bricks laid into the street, puddles glinting as if hiding riches you know couldn't possibly exist here.

The sounds of a lively, aggressive pub greet you as you draw up to the next junction (turn to **74**).

265

Clover Row comprises two series of tightly packed buildings that work down a higgledy-piggledy set of stairs. To your left you think you can hear the noises of some sort of sport. You wonder if it might be the Bradfell tradition of Privy, often played in the back rooms and rear courtyards of public houses across the city...in any case, you conclude it won't be as prestigious as the jousting and bear baiting Portsrood is known for.

The stairs lead you down to the city wall (turn to **80**).

As the first of the boggarts gets close enough, you swing your weapon wildly, making full contact and hearing the satisfying sounds of inhuman flesh being rendered lifeless by your hand. As you hit the second, the screams from passers-by fill you with pride at your righteous actions, until a forest of hands and arms suddenly envelops you, stopping you from defending yourself further.

"What are you doing?" a young man screams at you. "Guards, guards!"

Rapid footsteps behind you mix with the sobbing that now comes from every direction, and you are powerless to stop your hands being forced into a pair of secure cuffs at the hand of a local BLEED officer.

"It looks like we've found our murderer," you hear over your shoulder as you're marched away, and the crowd gets to work dealing with the blood of the innocent, with which you painted the streets.

267

The road simply – and aptly – named The Steep, doesn't pause its incline as it is met by Thrice Meadow Lookout, stretching away to the south-east. An almost pleasant-looking building has been set up where the roads meet, a sign over the door advertising it as "Lord Tunpet's Gambling Den".

Into the gambling den   Turn to **136**

North-east: The Steep	Turn to **205**
South-east: Thrice Meadow Lookout	Turn to **85**
South-west: The Steep	Turn to **278**

268

You call out that you need the toilet, and as if you're living in a children's story, the door opens to reveal a dumpy, middle-aged man.

"Oh, please stop shouting," he whines at you. "Alright, I'll untie you."

The ease with which you overpower him, tie and gag him, and untie your comrades, makes you question whether you've been set up. You cautiously peer out of the door to discover a small landing – you're not in a cellar, but in a converted roof!

Making your way down the stairs, it's clear the rest of the building is empty. As you descend to the ground floor and make your way outside, you're left wondering what that was all about, and if you'll ever get to know what they wanted with you.

"Thank goodness for that!" Sir Tostig says, clapping Sir Engelard on his back for his good idea. "Off we go, then!"

They each head off, leaving you alone again (turn to **116**).

269

The cobbled road heads up the hill in a slight zigzag, retaining the danger of the steepness while adding frustration to any cart drivers that find themselves at this point. A statue at the top of the hill combines with rainbow colours in your vision as you rise to meet another road (turn to 327).

270

The north-east corner of Brad Plaza offers a view to the east down the hill of Slumgate, and the northern slums that sit just outside the city wall at its base.

Built into the northern edge of Brad Plaza is a gate that grants access to Four Belly Gardens, while another road, Danger Alley, leads off to the north at its side. The short, narrow Downwards Passage offers to take you down a series of steps to the south-east.

The City Hall fills the eastern edge of the square, and a sign has been carefully placed to block the narrow alley that runs along its back wall, which reads "Warning! No entry!"

North: Danger Alley	Turn to 137
East: Slumgate	Turn to 338
South-east: Downwards Passage	Turn to 14
South: alley past the sign	Turn to 12
South: Politicians Court	Turn to 2
South-west: Travellers Court	Turn to 29
West: Preachers Corner	Turn to 161

271

Farewell Walk is a short road that smells like the rest of Bradfell: like sweat and sewage. The sooner you can get out of this dump, the better.

After only a couple of small buildings, you reach a Y-shaped junction (turn to **144**).

272

The gormless men seem to be wandering slightly less as you continue along Wall Street, gathering around various open doors and windows that form a string of watering holes to provide social interaction.

You find it hard to not judge them harshly for their lack of resilience, the poor incompetent fools, although you admit to yourself that the promise of a drink at some point does sound very tempting. Before too long, you arrive at another T-junction (turn to **130**).

273

You try not to slow down as you skilfully navigate your way through the crowds of people ambling aimlessly along, until you approach a city gate on your left.

Will you try to use the gate to lure the boggarts out of the city (turn to **341**), or keep on running (turn to **165**)?

274

This is a very steep climb. It isn't long before you start to regret your choice, but surrounded by locals you're not going to admit your discomfort. Remaining focussed on putting one boot in front of the other, you march up the hill until you reach the top (turn to **2**).

275 ☐

If you have the codeword *Foulon* and the box above is not ticked, put a tick in it now, and turn to **182**.

If you do not have the codeword *Foulon,* or if the box is already ticked, turn instead to **238**.

276

You look at Sir Julia expectantly, who looks back at you blankly.

"Oh, wait, this is it!" she suddenly cries, and then stares at you as if to accuse you of having messed up a plan she had been developing. "Yes, this one."

She leads you to an unassuming door set into the side of the building facing the gate, which is slightly ajar.

"Strange..." she murmurs, gently opening at leading the way in, up a winding flight of stairs and down a tight corridor to a door, hanging off its hinges.

Entering, you are greeted by a chaotic scene. A scruffy-looking bed in the corner is topped by a corpse, and a quick glance at Sir Julia is enough to confirm that it is Manfred's body. Clearly someone got here first and silenced a key witness to cover their tracks.

Manfred's home appears to be one room with a window facing the gate and a small washbasin next to it. A mirror that had presumably hung above the basin is broken across the floor, throwing shards of light against the cracked walls and a painting that, hanging at an angle.

The only other items of furniture in the room are a simple wooden chair, having fallen on its side, and a small, round table, upon which is a half-finished tankard of beer. An uninspiring selection of light brown clothes are strewn across the floor, mixing their shades with the varying browns put on display by the bare floorboards.

Investigate the body	Turn to **308**
Look out of the window	Turn to **287**
Investigate the crooked painting	Turn to **30**
Investigate the tankard of beer	Turn to **163**
Investigate the clothes	Turn to **360**
Leave	Turn to **226**

277

Thunder rolls overhead and you join in its audible grumble. At least Portsrood's shining walls glisten in the rain.

The cobbled street beneath your feet looks like tiny islands in a dull, grey ocean, and you're careful where you place your feet as you continue along Wall Street, reaching another T-junction (turn to **183**).

278

The hill keeps on falling, and you almost join it, having to grab onto someone passing as a cobble underneath your boots seems to rise out of the floor to trip you up.

Apologising to them and cursing the name of Bradfell, you angrily proceed until you reach the base of the hill (turn to **252**).

279

You don't stop moving, your boots crashing against the cobbled streets and reverberating against the walls as the crowds make way for you, apparently unconcerned about the catastrophe that's about to unfold.

After quite some time, you risk a glance behind you and satisfy yourself that you have shaken the creature off your tail. Heart still pounding and sweat dripping down your face, you look around you to get your bearings (turn to **80**).

280

The silver lining in the dark cloud of being killed through a blade slicing straight through your skull is a swift death.

Diving headfirst into Margaret's oncoming sword isn't the way you'd necessarily have chosen to die, but as your consciousness fades away you have to agree with the last words you hear: "It's going to take a while to clear up that mess, isn't it?"

281

Not for the first time since you've arrived, you begin to wonder why anyone thought it would be a good idea to build a city on a hill. Yes, it's visible for miles around, providing security and comfort to those in need both inside and outside, but it's an absolute pig to navigate. After some climbing, you reach a T-junction (turn to **267**).

282

Climbing this hill is even worse than it looked from below, making you at one point turn around to consider returning the way you came.

The nausea induced by looking down causes you to immediately turn around and hurry on up

– falling that distance on these rain-covered cobbles doesn't hold any appeal to you at all. Eventually, you arrive at another junction (turn to **95**).

283

You are the only person leaving Long Lane to step down this road that looks perfectly adequate, and look back for a moment in confusion.

Shrugging your shoulders and breathing in the sense of quiet, you head down the hill (turn to **167**).

284

You continue to lie there for a while, and still no-one comes. Turning to the wall, you notice some strange sigils carved in rows, and you can't help but begin to study them.

Your eyes are already drooping by the time you've studied the first, and you don't even finish looking at the details of the second before sleep has overtaken you.

You never wake up.

285

Well, this hill is significantly steeper than it looked like from the top. At one point you feel that it's so close to vertical that you find yourself having to grab hold of one of the ropes that line the houses here.

Thankfully, it is also short, and you are grateful to stumble onto the flatter Wall Street when you reach the bottom (turn to **357**).

286

The steps up this narrow alley aren't just steep, they're higgledy-piggledy, as if someone had dropped a pile of enormous matchsticks. Wondering how you've got there without falling, you reach the top (turn to **144**).

287

The view from here takes in the gatehouse with its disturbing imagery, but the height of Manfred's home gives a view out of Bradfell and over the countryside beyond the wall as well. The fields laid out across the plains remind you a little of the landscape outside Portsrood's own walls, and you are given a reminder that if you can solve this quickly then your route out of here will be that much faster.

Suddenly, your eyes catch the flap of a flag in front of you, and you have a brainwave. The flag is hanging from a rope that connects this house with the roof of the gatehouse in front of you, and by reaching up you confirm that it would carry the weight of a person. If whoever murdered Manfred entered through the window, maybe there are clues on the roof of the gatehouse...

Climb to the gatehouse roof	Turn to **322**
Investigate the body	Turn to **308**
Investigate the crooked painting	Turn to **30**
Investigate the tankard of beer	Turn to **163**
Investigate the clothes	Turn to **360**
Leave	Turn to **226**

288

If you have the codeword *Defarge*, turn immediately to **398**.

If not, turn to **361**.

289

The two guards separate from one another as you approach, nodding politely with a combination of respect and envy. You pass them and follow their directions up the staircase that stands immediately inside the door.

When you reach the top, another guard indicates that you should enter a bedroom, and walking in you find a space that screams out "crime scene". A little man with wispy hair is holding a notebook and carefully scribbling down words and pictures without interfering with the evidence, and as you come in he busily hurries the guard out and welcomes you.

"Hello there," he says, his voice a nasal staccato, "I'm Hugnym. I was told to expect you.

I hope you can be of help." He looks around himself, furtively. "You see, I visited Madame Sel last night and think one of her concoctions has disagreed with me. I don't learn, what? I seem to have lost the ability to read and write, which is rather irregular and a tad disruptive as I'm sure you appreciate. I don't like to be a nuisance, but do you mind taking a look at this list of suspicious items I've been making and see if you can give us something to go on?"

He hands you a barely legible list he's pulled together; you're going to have to compare his useless notes with the scene you can find in the bedroom.

Look at the list	Turn to **168**
Investigate the room	Turn to **363**
Leave onto Long Lane	Turn to **38**

290

The rain shows no signs of stopping, and you move as swiftly as you can through the storm. A door to your left suddenly bursts open and a woman violently pushes a man out of it and onto the ground, causing a great splash to rise up at your side.

"And don't come back until-" she shouts, and then stops herself short. "Ooh, it's a bit wet, intit? Come back inside, we'll finish this later."

The man pulls himself up and returns through the door, leaving you none the wiser. You plough on until you reach the end of the road (turn to 183).

291

"Alright!" he says, animatedly, "here's the plan. You and I are going to break into a house. But not just any house. A wizard has been dealing in magical items on the black market, so he's not going to report if any go missing. We'll split anything we find down the middle. You can keep them or sell them, that part's down to you. Meet me at the bottom of Memorial Lane. That's where my friend lives, so we can head over to the house together and break in."

Your new friend Orm saunters off, leaving you in your thoughts. Of course, the right thing to do would be to report him to BLEED, but if this wizard's dealing on the black market, maybe it's right for you to take matters into your own hands...

When you reach the bottom of Memorial Lane, the section will describe a house completely covered in ivy. When you reach that point, add 100 to the section number and turn to this new section number to knock on the door.

Record the codeword *Jacques*.

Stroll around the park	Turn to **129**
Leave onto Freedom Lane	Turn to **167**
Leave into Brad Plaza	Turn to **242**

292

Faraway Road starts steep, and seems to turn steeper up ahead. Trying to ignore the distracting murmurings of the townsfolk who teem around you as they pursue whatever interests Bradfell may have conjured up for them today, you press on until you reach a T-junction (turn to **135**).

293

The floorboard creaks out of place, and reaching inside the floor you pull out a piece of paper. Opening it up, you reveal it to be some sort of property deed. You pocket it for now.

Record the codeword *Bernard*.

Investigate the body	Turn to **308**
Look out of the window	Turn to **287**
Investigate the crooked painting	Turn to **30**
Investigate the tankard of beer	Turn to **163**
Leave	Turn to **226**

294

You approach the house and knock on the door, and after a few moments the door opens.

"Ah, welcome!" Orm says, opening his arm to gesture you inside. "My friend's just upstairs getting ready, let's head up there now."

You walk past him and up the stairs, and are greeted by half a dozen BLEED officers at the top.

"Ha!" one of them shouts. "I told you we couldn't trust anyone from Portsrood."

The whole thing was a setup, and as you're placed into chains you wonder how you're going to explain this to Queen Sophia, who's likely to have you executed for this bad behaviour...

295 ☐

If the box above is ticked, turn immediately to **51**.

If not, but if you have the codeword *Darnay*, tick the box above and then turn to **236**.

If the box above is not ticked and you do not have the codeword *Darnay*, do not tick the box, and turn instead to **310**.

296

As Wall Street continues, the crowd around you steadily changes from young women caring for their children into young men looking dazed and tired, simply staring into the middle distance as they pass one another. You wonder what might be having that effect, as the cries of the babies drift into your ears from behind you, and you reach a point where the road widens (turn to **252**).

297

If you have the codeword *Sydney,* turn immediately to **351**.

If not, turn to **28**.

298

One of the buttresses built into the city wall at this point juts out into the street, causing the constant churn of people and animals to get squashed onto one side. Glancing up, you see a pair of elderly locals sitting in rocking chairs and commenting on the chaos beneath them. Presumably this is what makes for entertainment in Bradfell.

You are grateful when you have left them all behind, and reach another road offering a route up the hill (turn to **318**).

299

You weren't sure what to expect when you started to shout again, but you didn't predict the reaction.

The ginger-bearded man wanders into your room, a bored expression on his face.

"Right then, you see, you, you, listen," he says, "I did warn you, didn't I? Mmm? Mmm?"

He's barely raised his hand before your vision suddenly goes entirely black. You raise your hands to check that your eyes are still present, but they don't reach your face before every bone in your body breaks simultaneously, causing you to collapse to the floor in a misshapen heap. The pain running through every ounce of your being takes a rapid turn for the worse, and your fully functioning nose begins to take in the smell of roasting meat.

You have been set on fire!

Unable even to move, you cry out a curse against all magic users before you pass out from the pain, never to wake up.

300

He stands as you approach, leaning on his crutch and waving the jug he was drinking from above his head. "How nice to meet you!" he yells, his eyes boring into your skull." My name's Edgar, and I was hoping to bump into one of you actually. You see, I'm quite well connected in this town, and could have a job for you. You interested?"

Will you say that you're interested (turn to 33), or say no (turn to 248)?

301

If you have the codeword *Carton*, turn immediately to 334.

If not, turn to 54.

302

"Alright then," he says, turning back to his paperwork.

What will you ask for now?

185

A necklace	Turn to **63**
A set of lockpicks	Turn to **349**
Sell something	Turn to **132**
Leave	Turn to **95**

303

A professional queueing system is in place to obtain a blessing, giving you a warm, fuzzy feeling inside. Regardless of what anyone might say about the despicable state of Bradfell culture, no-one can claim that they don't know how to queue.

When your turn arrives, you are welcomed into a comfortable, cosy booth with one of Husband Graham's wives to receive your blessing.

Unfortunately, the definition of the word "blessing" according to this place would appear to be different from any previous definition of it you've experienced. The "blessing" turns out to be a detailed and unnecessarily graphic story about an intimate experience the wife shared with Husband Graham recently.

When she's finished, you step out of the booth, bored, disgusted, and curious to investigate the extracurricular uses of a pestle and mortar.

What will you do next?

Speak to Husband Graham	Turn to **275**
Visit the herb garden	Turn to **110**
Leave into Black Dragon Grounds	Turn to **47**

Leave onto Wall Street   Turn to **194**

304

You quickly explain that you're well for the moment, and he expresses his happiness that that's the case.

"Well," he says, ushering you towards the door, "now you know where I am. I hope I don't have to see you again!"

You have to admit, it's good to know where a doctor is in this confounded city.

Leaving the physician, will you head to the north-west (turn to **175**), or to the south-east (turn to **213**).

305

You dig deep into your energy reserves and fly forwards as quickly as you can, batting the local residents away as you go and leaping through the air to tackle the fleeing man, landing on him as he collapses.

As he turns his head in shock to reveal a weaselly face with a thin moustache, you know you've made a mistake.

"WHAT ARE YOU DOING?" comes a scream from behind you, and you have no notice before the side of your head is suddenly beaten by something. Turning to look, you see a handbag hurtling towards you for another wallop. "That's my husband!"

Apologising profusely, you help the man up and back off, as a BLEED officer runs up to you, breathing heavily.

"Brannick got him."

You follow the officer to the City Hall, where Brannick is waiting with the now apprehended Husband Graham (turn to **400**).

306

"Alright," she replies, "well, you're in the right place. What sort of crime?"

You think for a moment, but have to admit that you don't actually have a crime to report. What will you do now?

Ask to speak to Brannick	Turn to **335**
Ask for information or equipment	Turn to **378**
Leave the building	Turn to **145**

307

The rain continues to bounce off your helmet and the floor in every direction as you tramp down the hill, sending splashes of water in every direction. At least in Portsrood the rain carries with it the freshness of the sea. Here it seems to act purely as a reminder of the grey lives these people lead.

You pause to shake the excess water from your boots as you arrive at a gate set into the city wall (turn to **108**).

308

The body is not attractive, although that's possibly because Manfred isn't your type more than the fact that he's dead. The body shows no signs of being beaten up that you can see; his hands and arms are covered in cuts and scars, but none look hugely new. The fact that he works as a butcher's assistant is enough to suggest these are from his work.

His neck also looks relatively clear, so it's unlikely he was strangled. Maybe he was poisoned?

Look out of the window	Turn to **287**
Investigate the crooked painting	Turn to **30**
Investigate the tankard of beer	Turn to **163**
Investigate the clothes	Turn to **360**
Leave	Turn to **226**

309

"I'll go the other way!" you hear Brannick shouting from behind you as you start to fight your way through the crowd.

Not too far ahead but gaining ground on you, you think you can see the back of Husband Graham's head, although you can't be certain it's him. Will you shout to the crowd to stop him (turn to **390**), or continue fighting your way through him to tackle him yourself (turn to **103**)?

The Phoenix and Pheasant is a classic tavern, with dark, wooden, high-backed benches forming clustered around tables along the exterior walls, a smattering of small tables between you and the bar, behind which an overweight woman sits precariously on a high stool.

"Alright?" she enquires as you enter, before immediately staring off into the distance, apparently expecting no reply. You comply.

The few locals that have set up camp at some of the tables look like they haven't moved from their current places for weeks. As one reaches up to rub his nose, you think you see dust falling from his sleeve.

Not wanting to spend too much time in this depressing place in case it's contagious, you toss a smile at the barkeeper and back out onto the Shaded Crossroads again (turn to **74**).

"I hear the footsteps of a brave knight!" comes a sudden crow from below waist height to your side. Sitting against the wall of a temple emblazoned with the name of The Sanctuary of Humility, an old beggar is shouting at you.

"I can't see you, but I can hear the sound of effective armour and a confident stride. I seem to have misplaced my cap; I don't suppose you could be so kind as to find it for me?"

Feeling enraged by her sense of entitlement to speak to you directly, you can't imagine what would bring you to take on some unimportant side quest, and then you see the cap sitting on the floor a few feet to her right.

Will you move it over to the crone with your foot (turn to **45**), or ignore her and continue on your way (turn to **352**)?

312

As she turns, you make your move towards her, preparing for a great punch into her mouth. She anticipates your move however, meeting your fist with her appallingly strong hand and pulling you towards her, causing her other fist to crunch into your face.

"Yes! I did it!" she yells. "Alright, I'll tell you where she is." She goes on to explain that Sir Julia was last seen passed out in Sophia Park.

Suddenly, her rage seems to kick back in, and she slaps a palm against one of the wooden partitions. "OH, I'M SO HAPPY!" she screams, before picking up a chair and hurling it across the room. It's probably time for you to leave.

Backing out carefully while rubbing your nose, leaking blood down your face and chest, you emerge onto the crossroads.

Record both codewords *Sydney* and *Stryver*, and turn to **74**.

313

The road begins to open up slightly as you follow it to the north, although the brightness promised by the bustle of Main Street is quickly countered by the drops of rain that begin to fall from above.

Narrowly avoiding the splashes from a puddle at the base of a drainpipe, you hurriedly reach the point where Wall Street reaches Long Lane (turn to 25).

314

The interior of The Shrine of the Trickle of Wisdom smells strange. Several small aqueducts flow in every direction, crossing one another and forming small waterfalls as scented water flows from one room to another.

A straw-haired man in a turquoise robe bows deeply towards you as you step through, before cupping his hand under some of the water and sprinkling it over his head.

Leave into Black Dragon Grounds Turn to 47
Leave onto the Shaded
Crossroads   Turn to 74
Leave onto Long Lane   Turn to 175

315

You mention the Fuming Fig to Sir Julia, and ask what conversation she was having there last night.

"Hmm," she thinks aloud. "Now, do you know what? That's a good question, isn't it? I can't remember. Take me there."

Record the codeword *Lucie* and decide where you will go next.

North-east: Faraway Road   Turn to **249**
North-west: Gait Gate   Turn to **344**
East: Clear Mist Lane   Turn to **234**
South: Wall Street   Turn to **130**

316

He smashes into you and you're not moved by the impact, but the ferocity with which he starts to scream at you, thrashing out with his tiny fists, is more than a little concerning.

"Take a punch, tin man!" he yells.

Will you use your strength to push him away and dive on top of him (turn to **243**) or swing your leg round to take his legs out from under him (turn to **106**)?

317

The dark, soot-covered stone of the Artificers' Quarter rising on either side of you, you navigate your way past piles of discarded goods and commodities, keeping your eyes fixed on the bright, crowded street ahead (turn to **340**).

318

You reach the T-junction at which Shepherd Hill, a narrow set of steps that creeps up towards the back of the City Hall meets Wall Street, which continues in both directions.

Clockwise: Wall Street	Turn to **124**
Anti-clockwise: Wall Street	Turn to **37**
West: Shepherd Hill	Turn to **286**

319

Leaving The Steep behind you, the crowd of young men begins to turn steadily into an equivalent crowd of young women. You look behind you, confused for a moment, and the people of Bradfell seem to have no awareness of this odd grouping. Deciding not to bother yourself with such trifles, you continue along the road until you reach another T-junction (turn to **109**).

320 ❏

If you have both codewords *Lorry* and *Manette* and the box above is not ticked, put a tick in it now, and turn to **188**.

If you have only one of those codewords or have neither, or if the box above is already ticked, turn to **224**.

You have to fight back the urge to express out loud your disgust at the colour scheme of Brown Alley. Why someone would decorate a street they lived on in this way is completely beyond you.

As if to turn insult to injury, a drop of rain falls onto the floor ahead of you, and then another on your helmet, and then you find yourself in a torrential rainstorm. This place is going to have a lot of explaining to do once you're done with it.

Desperately attempting the impossible task of keeping dry, you hurry on until you reach a crossroads (turn to **74**).

The rope swings a touch more than you'd like it to, but by fixing your eyes on your destination you are able to pull yourself across, the sounds of the people below drifting up towards you, muffled by the sound of the wind that funnels around you.

When you reach the other side, you make light work of pulling yourself up onto the roof, and a trapdoor in one corner gives you access inside the gatehouse; you climb down the ladder.

The room you end up in is full of about two dozen BLEED officers, who are less than impressed with your excuse for trespassing. Even you would have difficulty fending off this number of opponents, and so you don't try to struggle as they respectfully yet forcefully arrest you and march you out of the gatehouse, up Bradfell hill and to the City Hall.

When you get there, they take you to Brannick, the deputy chief of BLEED. He immediately apologises for the inconvenience without apologising for actually arresting you, and releases you.

"A word of advice," he says. "Can we try to limit the old lawbreaking while you're here, please?" Turn to **358**.

323

The view from this stretch of road is actually not unattractive, although the simple truth is that the only reason for that is that the view is of something other than Bradfell.

To the south-west, beyond the walls and the slums, a trio of open fields offer a delightful mix of colours, and the ripples of the wind passing through the flowers makes you yearn for the freedom of life on the road again.

Looking back the way you're walking, at the ignorant people and ugly buildings, you get a new sense of determination to get what you need done as soon as possible as you arrive at another road (turn to **267**).

324

You swing your clenched fist upwards, connecting precisely where you intended to but entirely failing to have the effect you were expecting, the huge man's flab acting as a cushion against your attack.

"Boo!" he shouts into your face, leaning into you in an attempt to push you backwards. "Fight me, you weakling!"

While this close to him you'll struggle to get an attack in. Will you suddenly duck down in an attempt to use his weight against him and tip him over you (turn to **217**), or will you viciously lift your knee up into his groin (turn to **196**)?

325

Continuing down Long Lane gives you the chance to experience one of the most up-and-coming areas of Bradfell, where the artificers on your right-hand side produce goods that the arty oddities on your left then adapt to remove their use and make them ornaments.

Ignoring the pretention, you make your way to a T-junction (turn to **175**).

326

The BLEED headquarters is a dismal place, drab wallpaper peeling away from the walls of the entrance hall, and rusty bars lining a small window in the wall, giving a glimpse through to the cells beyond. A pair of young women in uniforms that have also seen better days are casually discussing something from a pair of seats behind a large reception desk, and uniformed officers bustle around the place, apparently doing anything they can to look busy.

One of the women catches your eye, and with a raised eyebrow asks: "Are you in the right place mate?"

How will you reply?

Ask to report a crime	Turn to **396**
Ask to speak to Brannick	Turn to **335**
Ask for information or equipment	Turn to **378**
Leave the building	Turn to **259**

327 ☐

If the box above is ticked, turn immediately to **347**.

If not, put a tick in it now and turn to **35**.

328

Rain fills your consciousness as you start up the hill, and it's difficult to remember what the city was like this morning in the sunlight. A whimsical motif daubed on the building to your left does little to raise your spirits, although you wonder if you could transpose it to Portsrood somehow.

Still wondering about it as you climb the hill, you reach a point where the colour of the paving stones cause you to pause (turn to **95**).

329

No sooner have you reached the bottom of the wide, stone steps leading into Brad Plaza, a guard dressed in the immediately recognisable colours of Bradfell approaches.

"Ah," he says, "just the good looking, brave knights I was looking for." The three of you nod your heads in humble recognition at the accuracy of his statement. "If I might introduce myself? My name is Brannick." He bows with a dramatic flourish, causing you to jump in surprise, although you think you did a good job at hiding it. "I'm the chief of BLEED, the Bradfell Law Enforcement and Ethics Department."

"Wait," says Sir Tostig, "Isn't that Keegan? We met him last night."

Brannick clears his throat, his eyes awkwardly darting to the side as he does so. "Yes, well, I'm getting there. Truth be told, there is no chief at the moment. Keegan was found dead in his house this morning." Sir Engelard raises an eyebrow in curiosity. "As the deputy chief of BLEED, I'm...well...I'm deputising for him. We've not unlocked the gates this morning, so the murderer must still be within the city walls. You lot might not be trusted by everyone, but no-one will suspect you're working with us, so you might be able to get places that BLEED can't. Will you lend us a hand?"

The three of you share a glance, wordlessly concluding that the gates being shut are stopping you from getting out of here and back to Portsrood. You might as well see if you can help. You all nod at Brannick in agreement.

"Oh, thank you," he gushes, his relief palpable. "Keegan's house is just past Preachers Corner, you can't miss it." He points to the north-west corner of Brad Plaza. "I've already told the guards there to let you in, and you'll find Hugnym inside working his magic. I mean, I shouldn't use the word magic around him, he doesn't trust it as our chief alchemical investigator, but he does know his stuff and I'm sure will be grateful for your help."

With that, he passes you and trots up the steps to the City Hall, calling "Thanks again!" back at you.

Turn to **242**.

330

Record the codeword *Gaspard*.

The blue-purple flowers look a lot like acontro. You bend down to smell them, and yes, they smell of nothing. These must be what poisoned Manfred!

You get the attention of one of the wives in the garden and ask where else these might be available in Bradfell, and she confirms your suspicions: they are not available anywhere else. Finally, you're onto something solid. You ask if you can speak to Husband Graham, and she responds that he's not here. Apparently, he's gone to a meeting in Sumtumner Manor, the house in the middle of Sumtumner Grounds, to help Heidi think through the details of the new trade agreement with Portsrood.

To enter the house, add 150 to the section number you end up in when you reach Sumtumner Grounds.

Now, will you leave through the back into Black Dragon Grounds (turn to **47**) or through the front onto Wall Street (turn to **194**)?

331

A short, cobbled street connects the top of the Clover Row steps to Politicians Court (turn to **2**).

332

As you tread carefully through the shallow lake you find yourself traversing, an old man hurries past you, dragging a pig behind him. He ducks into a house and the pig follows him.

As he turns to close the door, he looks directly at you and unhelpfully says, "You ought to get in out of the rain," before slamming the door. The sooner you're done here, the better. The road takes you round a series of houses until you arrive at another T-junction (turn to **194**).

333

You are at a T-junction at which point Emerald Pass, an unassuming road leading up the hill towards Brad Plaza, meets Wall Street.

The crowd around you seems to favour wandering in Wall Street in both directions, although the odd person – some of them particularly odd, now you come to think of it – huff and puff as they realise they missed an earlier turn, and commit themselves to the climb.

North-west: Emerald Pass	Turn to **274**
Clockwise: Wall Street	Turn to **149**
Anti-clockwise: Wall Street	Turn to **133**

334

You easily get a helping of the water in your hand, taking a refreshing drink and filling up your bottle with it as well.

If you're ever asked if you'd like to use your water, multiply the section you are in by two, and turn to that new section.

Where will you go now?

Into the Travellers Rest	Turn to **198**
North-east: Velveteen Walk	Turn to **359**
West: Pride Pass	Turn to **399**
West: Thrice Meadow Lookout	Turn to **84**
To the Marked Gate	Turn to **201**
To Travellers Gate	Turn to **204**

The lady gets you to wait for a while as she shuffles out through a door, then returns and beckons you through and into a quiet room, before leaving.

Brannick is sitting on a wooden chair, staring up at a wall containing a map of Bradfell. Various locations have pieces of paper attached, connected by different coloured bits of string.

"Hi," he says, once your chaperone has disappeared. "Ignore this. How can I help you?"

Of course, you know that being told to ignore something means it must be important. You instinctively glance up, noticing only two pieces of paper. One, has been attached to The Saunter:

Legion Crushers?

Another is located in Four Belly Gardens:

Orm.

Will you ask him what led him to join BLEED (turn to 216), or if he can give you any helpful information about Bradfell (turn to 343)?

Otherwise, you can leave and ask the woman on the desk if you can report a crime (turn to 396), ask if they have any information or equipment you might find useful (turn to 378), or leave the building (turn to 259).

336

If you have the codeword *Lucie*, turn immediately to **215**.

If not, turn to **356**.

337

A few paces after having left Lonely Gate, the rain thankfully lifts and you are able to shake yourself at least somewhat dry. Aware of the locals wandering past you, you maintain the self-control to not curse at the top of your lungs.

Continuing clockwise along Wall Street, your steps bring you to Lowly Gate (turn to **226**).

338

You almost slip on your first step down the steep hill that is Slumgate. It takes its name from the city gate set into the wall at its base, from the time when the northern slum was the only one in and around Bradfell.

Halfway down, the residential houses on your left split, the carved stone above the gap announcing it to be the entrance to Sumtumner Grounds.

Enter Sumtumner Grounds	Turn to **229**
Continue to the bottom	Turn to **226**

204

The two sides of Long Lane at this point capture the two different sides of the city, both equally depressing. On your left are the workshops, their smoke and filth reflected most clearly in the people who toil in them, while the flamboyant art galleries and studios on your right seem to have lost all sense of reality, opting instead to float through life in expectation that love will conquer all.

Thinking to yourself that the only solution to the mindless work of the one and the idealistic drivel of the other is good breeding and chivalry, you reach a T-junction (turn to **340**).

340

Long Lane surrounds you in all its glory. Main Gate, a short walk to the north-east, used to bring travellers from far and wide, who would immediately dive into Artificers' Quarter to the south-west of here, or the Temple District to the north-east.

Afterlife Alley, appropriately named for its dull, smoke-covered visage, leads off into Artificers Quarter proper, while a narrow passage directly opposite it offers a route into Black Dragon Grounds, one of the city's green spaces. On the corner of this passage is a tall, narrow building, proudly bearing the title Portsrood Palace. You stare at it for a moment in disbelief; it shares as many characteristics with your home as the cobbles under your feet share with a pint of Hunwale Ale.

North-east: Black Dragon Grounds	Turn to **47**
South-east: Long Lane	Turn to **325**
South-west: Afterlife Alley	Turn to **231**
North-west: Long Lane	Turn to **52**

341

As you turn towards the gate, its flimsy wooden bars the only barrier between you and the outside world, a little voice in your head asks you why you would ever think this is a good idea, but you're committed now.

Running directly between the two guards flanking the gate, you leap feet first at it, bursting it open and landing, cat-like, before springing forwards to entice the boggarts to follow you.

The first crossbow bolt pings off your shoulder, but the second lands square in the small of your back, puncturing your armour and a kidney. You jerk to the side in pain, and a third bolt lands directly in the back of your neck, ending your life instantly.

342

You step into the ring, and the crowd around you starts to snigger quietly as the boy in front of you scratches his arm awkwardly, looking at you nervously. Hoping they are laughing at him and not you, the man who greeted you outside says, "Go on then," and before you have a chance to set yourself the boy begins to run at you.

Caught by surprise, you will have to react. Will you stand your ground and bring up your arms to block his run (turn to **316**), jab out at him with your fist as he approaches (turn to **68**), or make a move to hit him under the chin with an uppercut (turn to **107**)?

343

"What is there to tell?" he begins, as if the answer is "nothing", although that doesn't stop him from continuing.

"The city is built around Brad Plaza, the old market square where the old roads from Portsrood, Hunwale and Vanhelm originally met. The city itself is probably easiest to navigate by the big parks and the big pubs. So in the north, in the temple district, we have the Phoenix and Pheasant pub and Petal Meadows. And that isn't far from Sophia Park in the west, which leads down to the Fuming Fig in the south, and the Eager Griffon towards the town centre. The Travellers Rest is in the south, where you stayed last night, and the east has the nicest pub, the Duke of Vanhelm – it's where the well-to-do folk live, you know? Sumtumner Grounds is there, not far from and Four Belly Gardens is just to the north of Brad Plaza. Does that help?"

Unsure if it does or not, you consider what to do next.

Report a crime	Turn to **396**
Ask for information or equipment	Turn to **378**
Leave the building	Turn to **145**

344 ☐

If the box above is not ticked, and you have the codeword *Launay*, put a tick in the box now and turn to **382**.

If you do not have the codeword *Launay*, or if the box above is already ticked, turn to **97**.

345

You spin the little dial, listening to the clicks of the intricate machinery operating behind the door until a satisfying *chunk* tells you that it has successfully unlocked.

A smile breaking out on your face, you pull open the door, and time seems to slow down as what happens next is revealed to you.

The movement of the door causes the light to reflect on an almost invisible piece of thread, which your eyes follow up to the ceiling. A hidden tile on a hinge has swung open, causing a large vial of something to tip and spill down on you from above.

That's how the acid ended up covering your face and running into your eyes and throat. The searing pain instinctively causes you to try to scream, but the sound turns into a shrill warble as your vocal cords steadily shrivel, and you are burnt to death from the inside, the cackle of the hideous woman still playing on your memory as you pass.

346

The road seems to simply fall off the edge of Bradfell hill here, and you use the momentum to help you keep moving all the way to its base, skilfully avoiding a conversation with a group of locals as you do so.

A junction awaits you at the bottom of the decline (turn to 375).

347

The statue of Stanothy Pride still standing proudly above you, you feel a sense of urgency in deciding where to go next.

West: Pride Pass	Turn to 24
East: Pride Pass	Turn to 6
South: Lilting Lane	Turn to 153

348

Faraway Road is particularly steep here, made clear by the unattractive stream of some dark liquid flowing down the side of the street from Long Lane up ahead.

Avoiding treading in anything you would later regret, you continue until you reach another T-junction (turn to **320**).

349

"What?" he says, his eyebrows lifting almost to his hat, "Are you trying to get me shut down? I'm not allowed to sell lockpicks. Maybe in Portsrood that sort of thing's alright, but here I'd get into a lot of trouble for that."

What will you ask for now?

A necklace	Turn to **63**
A weapon	Turn to **91**
Sell something	Turn to **132**
Leave	Turn to **95**

350

It's only as you turn away from the Sanctuary of Humility that you realise the effect its bright whites have on the street. The buildings around the crossroads are all bathed in light, but as you move down the road you can almost feel your eyes gasping for light.

The eclectic mix of shops and other businesses along this stretch of Long Lane includes that of Physician Bottomley Pratt, and you make a mental note that his would be a good establishment to visit for medical aid.

You can visit the physician now if you wish (turn to **127**), or continue heading to the north-west (turn to **175**).

351 ☐

If the box above is ticked, turn immediately to **21**.

If not, put a tick in it now, and turn to **195**.

352

You feel bad for having ignored the beggar, but you can't please everyone, can you? You quickly look back to see if anyone else has lent her a hand in your absence, but both she and her cap have disappeared.

Presumably, she found her cap and moved off somewhere. Or maybe she was kidnapped. Never mind, you tell yourself, her poverty and blindness were probably her own fault.

Turn to **158**.

353

As you are about to step through the door, a voice behind you cries: "Hold it!" You think you recognise the voice but are unsure from where, and so you turn around carefully.

It's Orm, the man you met in the park, standing in-between two BLEED officers.

"So, you knew about a crime planned in the city and you didn't report it? That doesn't sound like the sort of behaviour we want in our city."

Before you have a chance to react, you are grabbed by the BLEED officers and marched into the cells. There's not much chance you're going to be able to get out of Bradfell now you're locked up in here...

354

Leaving the troll statue behind you, you follow Wall Street around a quiet corner, almost bumping into someone as they leave a house on the corner.

"Whoops! Don't mind me!" she blurts out without even looking at you, waddling in the direction of Troll Gate.

Almost as soon as you turn away from the rude woman, you reach another road leading away from the city walls (turn to 375).

355

The human hand and wrist are capable of some miraculous feats. The elven hand even more so. You heroically manage to shuffle yourself over to Sir Tostig, who is somehow able to use the slightest of gestures with his hand to pivot you up and onto his knees.

"Can you reach it?" he calls, and you kick your feet at the window, missing it narrowly.

"Ooh..." commentates Sir Engelard. "Just a foot more. Can you push him some more?"

"I think so!" Sir Tostig confirms. "Are you ready? One, two, three!"

He launches you, upside-down, towards the window. A touch too hard. You crash through the window, discovering immediately that far from being in a cellar, you are in a converted roof of a three-storey building.

Cursing as you fall, you provide the Bradfell locals with more gossip through the introduction of some new street decoration: a broken Portsrood Protector, still attached to a chair that itself somehow survived.

356

The Fuming Fig is the sort of place that passes for a classy establishment in Bradfell. The long bar area stretches out for quite some distance, and you count at least three servants gathering up glasses and making conversation with the punters.

The landlord is smartly-dressed, perched on a tall stool behind the bar, and nods at you as you enter. A quick glance around the room reveals an eclectic selection of drinkers at one end of the bar who look like they would welcome an addition to their group, and in the back room a group of ladies are playing the traditional game of Privy.

Speak to the landlord   Turn to **218**

Join the drinkers	Turn to **397**
Play a round of Privy	Turn to **176**
Leave north-east:	
Dragontoothache Passage	Turn to **234**
Leave south-east: Pride Pass	Turn to **222**

357

You have reached the base of Thunder Slop, an incredibly steep road that provides you with a commanding view of the back of the City Hall, an enormous banner bearing the Bradfell crest proudly hanging from its roof.

You pause for a moment to consider how awful the lives of the townsfolk here must be, that they seem to genuinely like this embarrassment of a city, but then decide it's a better use of your time to not think about it at all.

Wall Street extends in both directions from here, and a nice-looking inn bearing the name the Duke of Vanhelm sits on the corner.

Into the Duke of Vanhelm	Turn to **72**
Clockwise: Wall Street	Turn to **174**
Anti-clockwise: Wall Street	Turn to **298**
West: Thunder Slop	Turn to **159**

358

Bradfell City Hall is the grandest building in the grandest part the city. Robed officials march around you in pairs, discussing matters that are almost certainly unimportant but which apparently need discussing, and neither party wants to admit that they know the truth.

A pile of cloth caps bearing the crest of Bradfell sits in the entrance. You pick one up, and a helpful little woman suddenly appears, peering at you over a tiny pair of spectacles.

"Two gold pieces," she says. Of course, you are not carrying any money and so you carefully put the cap back and continue your exploration of the City Hall.

After a short walk around the building, which reveals nothing more of interest, you leave through the front door (turn to **131**).

359

If you have the codeword *Defarge*, turn immediately to **398**.

If not, turn to **122**.

360

The clothes are as normal and disappointing as you expected them to be, and none of them suggest that there is anything more to be discovered through carefully studying them.

As you make your way across them, one of the floorboards under the bed strikes you as being slightly skewwhiff. Perhaps it's just the way that people like Manfred have to live, or perhaps it's hiding something. You pull at it and it's definitely a little loose, although you'll have to properly break it open to see what's underneath.

Break open the floorboard	Turn to **293**
Investigate the body	Turn to **308**
Look out of the window	Turn to **287**
Investigate the crooked painting	Turn to **30**
Investigate the tankard of beer	Turn to **163**
Leave	Turn to **226**

361

The City Hall rising up to your left, you continue along The Saunter, a shaded, straight street that traditionally connected the south side of the city with the north. Halfway along the road, a line of lighter cobbles, barely visible now through the grime and horse excrement, mark the ancient boundary between north and south.

The road curves ever so slightly to the right, reaching a T-junction (turn to **185**).

362

Leaving Clear Mist Lane behind you, you find yourself entering a stretch of road lined with young men, clearly perfectly capable of work but are instead clustered around the buildings on your left, drinking and silently conversing. Ahead, the road opens up slightly (turn to **252**).

363

The room is a mess. The bed is on its side, revealing a mess that was underneath it, made up of half-eaten food, dirty plates, a bedpan, a razor and a book with the title Crime, Criminals and Criminality.

A desk set against the wall has only one fallen candle on top of it, while its drawers have been emptied out onto the floor: some quills, a BLEED badge, a telescope, a truncheon, a cleaver, pages covered in notes from investigations, a wig, a solitary shoe and a flyer for the theatre.

The only other item of furniture in the room, a wardrobe, has been opened and the clothes have fallen into a pile at its foot, including the BLEED uniform, a mask, a fake magic wand, a miniature dragon, a paperweight engraved with the word Bradfell and a handful of tissues.

If you know which item should not be here, take the letters that make up its name and turn them each into a number using the code A=1, B=2, C=3, etc. Add them all together and turn to the section bearing this number. If you are right, the opening line will contain the name of the item in question.

If you need some help, it may be worth looking at Hugnym's notes.

| Look at the notes | Turn to **168** |
| Leave onto Long Lane | Turn to **38** |

364

As you walk towards the hooded character, they suddenly twitch, giving you a glimpse of a slim face under their hood.

"Leave me alone!" they shout, leaping nimbly onto the table, grabbing onto the window ledge above them and squirming through.

The window is far too small for you, and you run outside to see them already some distance away.

Record the codeword *Jarvis*.

Will you give chase (turn to **67**), or simply let him go (turn to **98**)?

365

Faraway Road continues down the hill, the clattering sounds of cartwheels on the cobbles combining with the curses of those having to drive them up it.

It isn't long before you reach another T-junction (turn to **135**).

366

The rain pouring around you, you turn your attention to the wall and start to surreptitiously tap at the stones that make it up. You haven't been doing it for long when one moves, and when you're sure no-one's watching you try to shift it.

As if turning on a point deep inside the wall, the stone opens a door the size of a person, revealing a secret tunnel that seems to go under the wall!

Will you head into the tunnel (turn to **86**), or leave it for now (turn to **183**)?

367

The man marches purposefully through a door and into a back room, where four other men looking very similar to him are waiting.

"You've kept your face hidden for long enough!" one of them shouts, and without warning you find yourself in the middle of a whirlpool of flashing swords.

You defend yourself for several seconds, but the swordplay of these spies from the north finds its spot, and your life is ended swiftly.

368

As you begin to lean away from Gwendolyn's punch, time seems to slow down, and for the first time you notice that her arms are atypically long. As her fist connects with your face, an unpleasant crunching sound resounds in your ears, and the thought that this is not going to end well flashes across your mind.

You are pleased, therefore, to hear her guffaws, which both show that she is temporarily incapacitated and pleased with her result.

"I'll tell you!" she declares between laughs, before explaining that Sir Julia was last seen passed out in Sophia Park.

Suddenly, her rage seems to kick back in and she slaps a palm against one of the wooden partitions. "OH, I'M SO HAPPY!" she screams, before picking up a chair and hurling it across the room. It's probably time for you to leave.

Backing out carefully while rubbing your nose, leaking blood down your face and chest, you emerge onto the crossroads.

Record both codewords *Sydney* and *Stryver*, and turn to **74**.

369

The broad road leading down the hill towards the gate ahead is known as Freedom Lane. As you glimpse the Hunwale Mountains far off in the distance over the city walls, the thought of freedom strikes you more clearly than ever. The person who came up with this name was as observant as they come.

As you descend the mountains disappear from view. Then, as if to accompany the loss of this promise of liberty, a few spots of rain begin to fall. It becomes heavier, and when you finally reach the base of the hill, you are soaked through (turn to **108**).

The barman is friendly enough, and it doesn't take long to get him talking openly about the city.

"Oh, there's always plenty going on here you know," he says. "I'm sure Portsrood has its fair share of incidents in the court, but Bradfell has a certain...*shay mons prang*, if you catch my drift." He winks at you, leaving you wondering what he just said. "The latest I heard was of a secret passage at the bottom of Tortoise Walk, which takes you straight into the slums. If anyone's been causing trouble in the city, you can bet it'll be coming from there."

When you reach the bottom of Tortoise Walk, if you would like to search for a secret passage, multiply the section you are in by two and turn to this new section.

Greet the old man	Turn to **300**
Approach the shady character	Turn to **364**
Leave the Eager Griffon	Turn to **98**

371

You're caught off guard again by the ridiculous horn that blares its jolly sound at you as you step through the door. The slender shopkeeper leaps up from behind his counter, his neat goatee beard not stirring at all as he moves.

"Oh, hello!" he declares happily. "What would you like to buy?"

You have no money, and Sir Engelard turns ever so slightly towards you, mumbling, "We're wasting our time here..."

You can't disagree. You all leave, before you end up drawn into a conversation with this hindrance (turn to **80**).

(turn to **80**)

372

You share with the group the chain of clues you have pieced together, finishing with having found the acontro, at which point you look at Husband Graham.

"Yes!" he suddenly shouts, standing in a dramatic pose and flicking his hair over his head. "Yes, it was me. It was me! Manfred knew too much, he couldn't be allowed to live. He was the only one who knew I had the cleaver – well, he got it for me, didn't he? But Keegan, well, that was a matter of honour. Of spiritual honour, I say! My wives serve a holy purpose, they are there for the Husband's intimate pleasure, and he was taking advantage of them. He had even led Mandy astray to believe that she had fallen in love with him, removing her from the divine path. I had to maintain the purity of the Blessed House. It had to be that way, don't you see?"

All of a sudden, he turns and runs, diving straight through the window, sending jagged triangles of glass flying as if they were clearing his path through the air.

Instinctively, you give chase, comfortably slotting into the groove of pursuer of a quarry. He crosses Sumtumner Grounds at some speed, demonstrating the attractive leg muscles you noticed when you first arrived, and out onto Danger Alley, but you lose sight of him as he runs into a crowd of people heading to your left. You can't tell which direction he's gone.

Will you run to the left, following the crowd (turn to **381**), or to the right, fighting against the flow (turn to **309**)?

373

You plant your foot firmly into her back and she collapses forward, knocking over a table and landing in a heap.

"Well, fair's fair," says Oswald, "your friend was here last night, with young Tom. Tom's here actually, perhaps she's still around. TOM!"

A young man emerges from the kitchen, drying his hands on his apron. You have to admit, he's surprisingly handsome for a place like Bradfell.

"That knight you had draped over you last night, she still here?" asks Oswald.

"Naw," says Tom, "we went for a walk to Sophia Park but then she fell asleep on the grass and I couldn't wake her up, so I just came home."

"NOT FAIR!" comes a sudden scream from behind the toppled table as Gwendolyn stands up. "YOU DON'T KNOW HOW TO FIGHT!"

She launches herself at you but stumbles into the table, tripping over and falling again. Her rage becomes louder, and you swiftly make your exit while the sound of carnage continues behind you.

Record the codeword *Stryver* and turn to **74**.

374

"In fact, he was getting very friendly with one of your friends. You know, the one with the beard."

When you explain that Sir Julia is currently a little indisposed, he chuckles. "Not unexpected for her to be the worse for wear after the way she was behaving last night, now I come to think of it. Oh, excuse me."

He follows the call of duty to help his staff change an ale barrel, leaving you alone at the bar. It appears that finding a cure for Sir Julia is even more important than you thought it would be, you're going to have to prioritise that now.

Record the codeword *Gabelle* before deciding what to do next.

Join the drinkers	Turn to **397**
Play a round of Privy	Turn to **176**
Leave north-east:	
Dragontoothache Passage	Turn to **234**
Leave south-east: Pride Pass	Turn to **222**

375 □

If box above is ticked, turn immediately to **333**. If it is not ticked, put a tick in it now and turn to **39**.

376

Wondering why you've agreed to go ahead with this lunacy, you allow yourself to be placed onto one of the little carts and weigh the blade in your hand as you're blindfolded. You're still mulling your life choices over in your mind when the whistle blows, and you scrabble your feet along the floor to get yourself moving.

The room is reasonably long, and so you get up some speed before you think you're approaching Margaret. Will you swing your blade to your left (turn to **394**), or to your right (turn to **27**), or will you dive forward out of the cart, hoping to duck underneath their blade and catch them full on (turn to **280**)?

377

You begin to step down the hill, the change of hues giving you almost a bodily sensation as the vivid colours of Brad Plaza fade into the moody blacks and purples of Velveteen Walk. The array of small craft shops and homes on either side of you bring with them a particular brand of creativity and incense that makes you feel distinctly uncomfortable, making you long for the comfortable predictability of Portsrood.

Just as the sounds from the crowds at Brad Plaza are starting to die down, more fill your ears from ahead, and the bottom of the hill takes you into Travellers Place (turn to **36**).

378

"The biggest thing newcomers into Bradfell miss is the warning signs around Freedom Lane. The Twisted Pixies set up a little hostel there some years ago, and attack anyone who gets too close on sight. Just steer clear of that area and you'll be fine."

Grateful for the information, you consider what to do next.

Ask to speak to Brannick	Turn to **335**
Report a crime	Turn to **396**
Leave the building	Turn to **259**

379

You confidently march across Sumtumner Grounds, right up to the front door of the house in its centre, and knock loudly.

A few moments later, the door opens and you are welcomed in, straight through to a room containing Heidi, Husband Graham and BLEED deputy Brannick, along with another half dozen or so important-looking people.

Now, if you have the codeword *Ernest,* turn to **119**.

If not, turn to **372**.

380

Leaving Lonely Gate behind you, you begin the long march up the hill, the buildings on either side of this wide road facing off against each other as if in conflict over whose side of the city is better.

A young lady stops you on your climb. "I hope you're enjoying your time in Bradfell!" she squeals in mock coyness. "Make sure to visit Lord Tunpet's Gambling Den while you're here, there's always fun to be had when money's on the line!"

Leaving her ravings behind you, you reach another junction (turn to **167**).

381

"I'll go the other way!" you hear Brannick shouting from behind you as you start to fight your way through the crowd.

Not too far ahead but gaining ground on you, you think you can see the back of Husband Graham's head, although you can't be certain it's him. Will you shout to the crowd to stop him (turn to **126**), or continue fighting your way through him to tackle him yourself (turn to **305**)?

Edgar is waiting for you as you arrive, and he waves at you in greeting.

"Look at all these people!" he says, gesturing with his arm to show a rabble of children he seems to have conjured up for the purpose of this demonstration. "I didn't have to do anything, the Council came and found me right after you did!" he pulls his hand out of his pocket, brandishing a piece of paper you recognise as the forged deed. "Come on, let's head over there now."

He begins to march up the hill and you go with him. Along the way, he stops at every child he sees, pausing for a brief conversation and adding to the crowd of orphans he seems to have gathered.

When you reach the Portsrood Palace building, you recognise the two children you met before standing outside, and the look on their faces is worth the effort it took you to get here. Edgar greets them warmly before unlocking the front doors and ushering all of them inside.

"I know it's not much to look at," he says, while the shrieks of the children exploring their new home bounce off the walls around you, "but you know you've just transformed the lives of dozens of people. I can't say any more than just thank you, on behalf of the next generation of Bradfell."

Your heart feeling slightly confused by this new sensation of having helped people purely out of the goodness of your heart, you can't help smiling, and back out of the new orphanage with a new lease of life (turn to **340**).

383

Faraway Road rolls downward towards one of the city's lesser gates set into the walls. It seems as if the city becomes even grimmer the further you get from the centre, and your desire to get out of here increases as you reach the bottom (turn to **344**).

384

Edgar is waiting for you as he promised, and greets you as you approach.

"Ah, you found me, good work. Now, did you get the deed?" You take it out and show it to him. "Brilliant, that's the one. Now, listen carefully. That deed is to a house on Long Lane called Portsrood Palace, right on the junction with Afterlife Alley. The owner died, and I have a plan to turn it into a lovely orphanage but the town wants to turn it into something awful and boring, I'm sure. If you take that deed to my friend the Green Teabag, he'll forge a copy of it in my name. Then all we'll need to do is break into Portsrood Palace and plant the evidence. In the master bedroom, there'll be a dresser containing one large drawer. Put the forged deed in there, then when the authorities are looking for it they'll come and find me! And talking of finding me, if you ever need to, my house is just next to Lonely Gate."

He explains that the Green Teabag is located at the bottom of Resolution Hill, through a door marked with a symbol, which apparently is meant to represent a coin but looks more like an orange. When you think you have reached the Green Teabag's hideout, add 45 to the section number you are at and turn to this new section.

When you reach Portsrood Palace, if you would like to break in then deduct 200 from the section number you are at and turn to this new section.

Slapping you confidently and entirely inappropriately on the back, he marches off, leaving you to your thoughts (turn to 237).

385

The unstoppable swell of people who use Wall Street for travel and, inexplicably, socialising, when other areas in this awful city are substantially less grim, begins to take on a different look and feel as you follow it around the city wall.

A horse trots past you in the opposite direction with no rider, and you could swear it nods in recognition at you as it goes. You quickly move towards the bright space ahead, which looks like Travellers Place (turn to 201).

386

You are in The Blessed House of the Husband of Countless wives and Sagas of Courageous Acts With Said Wives.

The Blessed House of the Husband of Countless Wives and Sagas of Courageous Acts With Said Wives is a large, multi-storey, intricate building, full of corridors and small rooms. The walls and furniture are all pristine, and the smell of fresh food wafts through every space you explore here.

This is the spiritual and physical home of Husband Graham, along with his many wives, of which there are dozens. All dressed in white robes, their primary activity seems to be to talk to one another, while the brown-robed servants, almost all of whom are suspiciously good-looking men, hurry around doing the chores.

Speak to Husband Graham	Turn to **247**
Get a blessing from a wife	Turn to **157**
Leave into Black Dragon Grounds	Turn to **47**
Leave onto Wall Street	Turn to **194**

387

The Blessed House of the Husband of Countless Wives and Sagas of Courageous Acts with Said Wives, almost shimmering in the rain, is almost as large as its name is long, and the tittering sounds of stories being told within its walls float through the rain towards you.

You hurry forward, past several other buildings with no names as far as you can tell, until you reach the Main Gate (turn to **25**).

388

Leaving Travellers Place behind you, you follow the city wall as it slowly bends around to the left, presenting you with a T-junction after only a few buildings (turn to **375**).

389

The rain is not letting up, and you splash through puddles alongside a row of houses that, now you've seen them in the rain, you can't imagine not looking as grim as the refuse piles you passed on your way into the city.

A particularly murky corner seems to await you in the distance, and you pause as you reach a T-junction (turn to **183**).

390

At your shout, one of the heads in the crowd suddenly seems to grow, and a body unfurls itself to reveal an enormous troll, a sneer breaking out across its face. Reaching one massive hand out, it stops Husband Graham in his tracks, and you soon catch up with him, along with a handful of BLEED officers, who put him under arrest.

"Thank you," says the troll in a deep, rounded tone, trying to string more than two syllables together. "Bradfell is a hard place to live as a troll. I've struggled with racism ever since I got here. But today, I've been the hero."

Ignoring his meaningless prattling, you follow the BLEED officers to receive the reward for having saved the city from a murderer in its midst (turn to **400**).

391

Wall Street becomes quite narrow at this point, the shadows giving it a foreboding presence, although the rain seems to stop as you're walking, the brightness that creeps around the buildings ahead powerful in its ability to lift your spirits.

Enjoying the feeling of the sun again, you step deeper into the Artificers' Quarter, and after you've passed several small shopfronts, you reach a T-junction (turn to **65**).

392

You are approaching the corner of the City Hall when a movement above you causes to glance upwards. You suddenly scream involuntarily, as the full breadth of the dragon begins to block out the sky, its neck rearing back as if to about to roar – or worse, breath flames all over you.

Unable to control yourself, you scream and begin to run away, the whole time hearing your inner monologue having an argument about how you're meant to be a brave knight and that this sort of thing is your bread and butter. You gallop down a hill away from Brad Plaza without thinking, reaching a T-junction at the end. Will you turn left (turn to **121**) or right (turn to **279**)?

393

You have to shield your eyes from the bright sunlight reflected off the impeccably white building on your right as you climb up Faraway Road. Looking over your shoulder as you near the top, you wistfully gaze at the outside world, becoming increasingly impatient to get out of Bradfell.

Hunching your shoulders, you push yourself forward until you arrive on Long Lane (turn to **213**).

394

You swing to your left but do not connect, and the feeling of your opponent's blade slicing almost clean through your arm seriously smarts. You collapse in a heap, your blood pooling on the floor around you.

"Ha ha!" you hear Margaret's voice ringing out. "How do you like that, loser?!"

Slowly losing consciousness, you're aware of hands dragging you onto a stretcher, and Margaret saying, "Come on, weed, let's get you to the temple." You pass out.

When you come to, Margaret is nowhere to be seen and it takes you a few moments to realise where you are (turn to **314**).

395

This portion of Wall Street is one of its busiest, with people pushing past you in both directions. The building on this corner is ornately decorated with pictures of what look like bears with the heads of dogs, although the more you look, the less convinced you become that they're not dogs with the heads of bears.

You pull your gaze away from them and towards the next junction (turn to **318**).

396

If you have the codeword *Jacques*, turn to **59**.

If not, turn to **306**.

397

You approach the few people gathered at one end of the bar and introduce yourself.

"I hope Bradfell's treating you well," a middle-aged lady with streaks of grey in her curly hair says to you. "It's always a pleasure to meet someone from Portsrood. Actually, maybe I could entice you to become a customer? I sell bottles, you see, and it would be lovely for my little business to say I count one of the Protectors as a customer."

The truth is, you have no money and so couldn't become a customer even if you wanted to – and so you explain this to her.

"Aw, that's a shame. Well, maybe you can do something else in exchange for a bottle. It would be helpful if you'd settle an argument we've been having, then I'll give you one for your trouble. You see, Jinfried here just bought a round." She indicates a short man with a thick beard as impressive as Sir Julia's, who turns to you and mumbles something you don't catch. "He made a joke about the fact that the cost of the round was just a rearrangement of the money he had on him – like, he had 542 Jimmies on him and the round cost 245. Anyway, the change he got then turned out to be another arrangement of those numbers, and then he spilled all his money all over the table!"

The man introduced as Jinfried rolls his eyes at his own clumsiness and mumbles something else you're not able to make out. How he was able to communicate the rearrangement of digits in a financial transaction is beyond you.

"We're trying to make sure he's got the right amount," the lady continues. "I don't suppose you can help?"

Can you work out how much money Jinfried should have? The answer will be three digits long. If you can work it out, multiply those three digits together and turn to the section bearing that result.

If you can't solve the problem, you'll have to apologise and choose to do something different.

Speak to the landlord	Turn to **218**
Play a round of Privy	Turn to **176**
Leave north-east:	
Dragontoothache Passage	Turn to **234**
Leave south-east: Pride Pass	Turn to **222**

398

You have only taken a few steps away from the junction when you inexplicably collapse to the floor, your head spinning. A stranger leaps to your aid, asking you what the matter is, but every attempt you make to speak leads only to meaningless groans that do little more than reveal the pain and confusion you suddenly find yourself in.

Before you know it, your eyes are drifting shut as your heart and lungs steadily slow, and then stop entirely.

399

The bustle of the open space behind you turns into a different, frustrating sort of busyness as you begin to traverse Pride Pass. The man after which this road was named, Stanothy Pride, championed the rights of the poor, a fact the local folk seem to celebrate for some reason, and the slogans and images lining the street steadily anger you more and more as you arrive at a truly infuriating junction (turn to **327**).

400

"Thank you!" beams Heidi, a little red-faced from the walk up the hill but covering it well with her enthusiasm. "All's well that ends well and all that. And I'm glad you found your friend, I'm sure she'll think twice before having another of those nights again!"

Sir Julia mutters something through her beard, although rather than gratitude or repentance you wonder if it was her asking when the celebratory drinking will begin.

"But now," continues Heidi, "we have a new predicament: who is the rightful heir to the Husband's House? Tradition would state that the one who bested the Husband is next in line, and so that would be you. Would you like the job?"

The thought of having to spend any more time in this backward outdoor prison gives you a sudden urge to punch her in the face, but you manage to hold yourself together and politely decline.

Having gathered your things together and mounted your trusty steeds, you and the rest of the Protectors trot out of Bradfell and head east.

Sir Engelard wonders out loud what you all might do to pass the time as you travel, and Sir Julia mentions that she'd heard of a bandit's redoubt not too far to the south of here that might threaten Bradfell.

You discuss it for a moment, but quickly conclude that you all deserve a break from this excitement. Sharing stories of what you've missed of Portsrood, you continue onward, the warmth of the sun on your back, and the glimmering promise of home ahead.

About the author

Family man. Collaborative storyteller. Jesus follower. Executive coach. Author.

None of us are only one thing.

Get to know Samuel better – and have a look at his other gamebooks – on his website:
IsaacsonAuthor.com

Printed in Great Britain
by Amazon